THE LITTLE ILIAD

SECOND EDITION

THE LITTLE ILIAD

BY
MAURICE HEWLETT

WITH A FRONTISPIECE BY
SIR PHILIP BURNE-JONES

PHILADELPHIA & LONDON
J. B. LIPPINCOTT COMPANY
1915

COPYRIGHT, 1915, BY J. B. LIPPINCOTT COMPANY

PUBLISHED SEPTEMBER, 1915

PRINTED BY J. B. LIPPINCOTT COMPANY
AT THE WASHINGTON SQUARE PRESS
PHILADELPHIA, U. S. A.

"There were four brothers loved one lass."
—CORMAC AND STANGERD

CONTENTS

THE LITTLE ILIAD

I

INITIATION

I AM sure that such things as I have to relate
in these chapters—things of which I was the
concerned witness from beginning to end—
could not happen in any country of Europe
but my own, a country where respect for things
in being is carried to the other side of idolatry,
and where, at the same time, you may see
men, and even communities of men, run head-
long down steep places to destruction in pursuit of abstract ideas, and win in the ridiculous
act the admiration and respect of those to
whom the ideas themselves are shocking. A
Briton, you admit, reveres established order,
fears God, honours the King, loves his father
and mother, &c. So he does. But say that
a man knocks his head against established
order—sufficiently hard; say that he perishes
for atheism's sake, is exiled for his nihilism,
disputes his father's will, to bankruptcy, or
runs away with his neighbour's wife on altru-

9

istic grounds—that man, when he has been disposed of with savagery, may easily become a national hero. We say that it's dogged that does it, that he is a True Blue, a hard-bitten man. If he is a poet, he becomes a classic. If he is a politician, he founds a party, and his name inflames men to dangerous cheering. To be short, we adore the thing that is, because it is; and we adore the man who tries to destroy it, not because he succeeds, but because he tries. It's all very odd.

But sentiment, which in England carries its head so high, carries also lance and shield, and presents a brave front to the wind and the rain. The harder, indeed, it blows, the more bravely pricks the gentle knight. It is fair weather that brings him down. For he carries with him, too, his own bane; a little worm which gropes a way into his marrow, and inflames the optic nerve.

When Hector Malleson went out to set the world into order it was not riot or clamour that loosened his knees. On the contrary, the extreme lengths to which the romantic led him were in themselves a warrant of success. He was in fact too successful. All

fell out as he could have desired. He achieved
a preposterous position for himself and his
mistress. He bestrode a bottomless gulf with
triumphant intrepidity. The world wondered.
And then, even as we gaped, he sagged in the
middle and fell in. The affair which he had
begun went on of itself. It was as if the
champion of Troy, instead of going out to
face Achilles, had stayed at home with the
toothache, and left the affair to Priam, King
and Patriarch. That was what happened in
this leaguer of a minor Troy, which I chronicle
here. A maggot entered my poor Hector and
palsied his blow. You see, I scorn conceal-
ment. I lay out my wares on the tray. I
could even tell you the name of the maggot,
but that you have guessed it for yourself.

I remember talking about these very things
to Hector Malleson on one of our annual
journeys over the Continent, of which Great
Britain is so discordant a member—long before the events which I am going to write
about now were in solution. We were driving
up and down those huge circular sweeps of
road which take you in time, though you don't

at the time believe it, over the Jura; and were
talking, to be exact, about the power of love
to "make or mar the foolish fates." Hector,
dear, absurd fellow, was one of those men
who when they are in love cannot conceive
that they ever were or ever will be out of it
again, and when they are not (which happens
quite as often) do not believe that they ever
were. At the moment he was not in love;
he had, in fact, just escaped a rather bad
attack in London with a young and very pretty
widow, a black-haired woman with a mag-
nolia-skin and the appurtenances thereof. She
sailed, rather suddenly, to Buenos Ayres, and
left him like Ariadne in Naxos. It was tonic.
He shook himself, shuddered, and foreswore
love.

Now, in the Jura, he was telling me with
all seriousness that no great man, "no man
born to great destinies," as he put it, had
ever risked his greatness for a woman. Not
being concerned to affirm or deny, I didn't
go far afield for my example, but mentioned
Paris, the "woman-haunting cheat," who is
surely the type. Paris, of course, will only
support a very light-hearted argument; but

he took him on for more than he was worth,
being Hector Malleson; he took him histori-
cally, and disposed of him thus. "Paris,"
he said, "is obviously your man"—as if I
wanted a man!—"but he won't help you.
Paris, to begin with, was not Priam's heir.
Hector was the heir. I think that is obvious in
the name given to his son by the people—Asty-
anax, they called him: King of the city. That
was proleptic. That is allowed in poetry."

I said that he ought to know—for he was
by way of being a poet himself. That also
he took gravely, and I remember how he sat,
with an outline something between an inter-
rogation and an exclamation-mark, drawn up
stiffly to his slim height, with his hands pointed
between his knees.

"Paris has been misunderstood," he said.
"He has been taken for a sensualist, but
wrongly. He was a great idealist. He risked
his father's kingdom and dared ten years of
war for the sake of an idea. Now that's a
very different sort of thing. Many a man
has been eaten by worms for that—but not
for love." I felt rather than heard the tremor
in his voice.

"And what was Paris's idea, according to you?" I asked him.

He replied immediately. "The profanation of Beauty. He risked everything to prevent that. And he was right. If he had been Crown Prince of Troy he could have done no less."

Now Hector was a Crown Prince in his way. He was the eldest son and heir of Sir Roderick Malleson, Bart., of Singleton and Inveroran, in the Western Highlands—to the permanent bewilderment, let me add, of that royal-eyed old Berserk himself. So you may say that he measured his words. But he always did that. He was the most serious young man in the world, and one of the most ridiculous. Men of extreme positions—and he was one of them, forever at the end of the bough or the top of the pole—must always appear that to us who are snugly by the hearth. It is gallantry that carries them there, and only human nature that makes them see-saw for a balance. But the effort is ungraceful, and we smile.

I was awfully fond of Hector. He was as good as gold, as the saying is. But he was

the cause of infinite chucklement to me, and
sometimes he brought me tears—or something very much like tears.   Himself, he
never laughed.

I remember that conversation perfectly, and
can see him with his thin olive face and heavy
eyes, his slim gallantry and air of a lost cause
—only too well.   But it took place many years
before we met the von Broderodes.   Many
things happened to Hector Malleson in the
interval; many a touch-and-go affair was
hit upon and just missed; many a stormy
interview with Sir Roderick flashed and vol-
leyed through Inveroran, and died away in
mutterings among the hills up there.   They
made a great rumpus at the time, and had
Hector at the edge of the world contemplating
infinity with tragic eyes as often as you please;
they divided the great patriarchal house into
hostile camps, so that sometimes you had
Hector and half of his brothers breakfasting
and dining in the East Wing, while his father
and a remnant held the wall, like a citadel,
and commanded the supplies.   There was one
occasion—I mean when Mrs. Gellaghtly, a
sprightly American, was there.   She lifted her

fair foot once and struck a match on the sole
of her shoe. One saw—well, one had to look
out of the window. And then she got lost
in the forest with Pierpoint and came back
to breakfast as if nothing had happened—
as perhaps it did not. There was that one
occasion, I say, when I really thought the
House of Inveroran was rocked to the foundations. Hector, who had brought the lady
upon us, had gone bail for her, you may say,
and even at this eleventh hour was her champion, shook the dust off his brogues and
vanished; two of his brothers went with
him. The situation was saved by Mrs. Gellaghtly herself, who did *not* vanish—and by
Mr. Gellaghtly, an elderly, very thin person
in a frock-coat and white tie, who came and
lived unmoved through an electric twenty-four
hours. She called him "hub" and perched
upon his narrow knees. She was like—or
looked like—a speckled hen sitting on a fence;
it was daring, and entirely successful. Sir
Roderick simmered down, Hector wrote a
long letter on foreign notepaper from Madeira,
or somewhere of the sort, and all was peace
again. He came up to Inveroran for Christ-

mas. That was the last of his eruptions for
at least a year and a half. Indeed, affairs had
gone with perilous smoothness up to the spring
when we were abroad together, and met the
von Broderodes. Then, indeed, the casting
of threads began which were to involve us
all in a pretty plexus. To that I must now
address myself.

The thing began in a watering-place, to
call it so, in the South of Central Europe, in
a place which I need not particularize further
than by saying that on the edge of a beautiful
lake, under the guard of solemn and slumber-
ous mountains, the greed of man to secure
the shillings of his stupid fellows has done his
worst to soil the one and flout the other. The
description, I confess, is general; but I don't
care to go any closer to it for obvious reasons.
The thing began, as such things, in my
belief, always do begin, in a flash. A blink
of the eyes and there is nothing; a blink of
the eyes and there is this life and the next,
the hope of heaven and the yawn of hell.
How is it that at one minute you are looking
at familiar things—ducks in a pond, a man

2

and woman talking, a boy in a bath-chair
and a girl walking beside it—and at another
you see upon them the light that never was?
What has happened that the heart is touched,
trembles to tears? The thing is done, all
your life-scheme is changed. What sudden
glory floods your day with the implication of
God? What stab of the heart brings it about
that you are not the man, nor she the woman,
you were a moment ago? Whence comes a
glory upon her, a sanctity? The particles,
the flesh and bone, the hair and skin have
been rearranged, transfigured. You yourself
now thrill like an Æolian harp; and as for
her, she is garmented with light. There's no
explaining a thing of the sort. It is not—
and then it is. It has never been so yet to
me. My time's to come. But it happened
to Hector about once a year. He was a great
hand at miracles.

I had been at this place—let us call it
Gironeggio at once and have done with it—
with Hector Malleson for a week or so of fine
April weather: misty mornings clearing to
burning noons, weather of magnolias in a

riot of bloom, of corn already knee-high, of
blue fields of flax, of roses dusty with the
foul traffic of man in his roads. There was
nothing to do but be glad of it all, take it all
in through the pores. One felt, after a London
February and March, as if one had earned
it. I think we intended to have another ten
days there at least before we addressed ourselves to the small cities of Lombardy, where
I intended to archæologize and Malleson to
read history. If only he had read history
instead of made it! But you never know your
luck. There were Modena and Parma and
Cremona gaping for him—and he must choose
the primrose path!

However, Gironeggio was very pleasant, and
the particular Majestic Palace where we were
lodged was better than most, being, in fact,
less majestic. But it was full. The English
were, as usual, mostly of two professions.
Every one of them seemed to be either bar-
rister or schoolmaster; all of them were engaged in climbing the mountain or collecting,
with avid haste, plants which they could slay
at their leisure in Thames-valley or Kent-
coast rockeries. They were a brisk and

wholesome company, but not illuminating,
unless you like your light very dry. Their
wives, short-skirted and clump-soled, flat
of figure and tanned of face, accompanied
them, severe and uncompromising matrons
with views as decided as their petticoats. I
liked their daughters best, who looked like
boys all day, and dressed for dinner as if they
were going to a children's party afterwards.
Malleson got on well with them, because he
was perfectly serious and had no self-con-
sciousness. They, having enough for six,
found him easy. The rest of our company
were Germans; but of them, so delightful at
home, so devastating abroad, with their
exaggerated politeness and latent brutality,
I must speak with reserve—because we became involved with Germans. We found out
for how little race counts when the particles
have been rearranged by the Lady Fates—
and also for how much.

But people fall easily into types; and for
a week neither Malleson nor I took the trouble
to get them into narrower categories. Every
fat man with a rolled neck who made jokes
and punctuated them with bowing salutations

from the hips seemed to be German; every
dark man with large ears and handsome and
bulky ladies attached to his person we took
for a Jew; every man with a ragged beard
and mild eyes was a Russian . . . and so
forth. When you came to know these people
well enough to take liberties with their faces,
you could sort them out. By a process of
weeding you discarded the uninteresting or
the obvious. And just as, by gazing steadily
into the dusk, things emerge which you did
not remark at first encounter, so it is with
a crowd of people: a face suddenly looms
and seems to cry to you. And then, in a
minute, you are hard up against a mystery
or a romance.

Now all this preamble is to explain how
it is that a couple of people in that hotel had
been in front of us for a week of days before
we considered them, or so much as knew they
were there. When I did become conscious of
them I judged that they had been there some
time. They had the air of habitués. They
seemed to have cushioned out for themselves
corners in the rigid discomfort of our majestic
palace. They always occupied the same places

at the same hours. The waiters brought them, without orders, the same things at the same moments every day. Her egg-and-milk at ten-thirty: she took it in the garden. At eleven she gave *him* her arm and took him off to walk. She had tea and lemon at four; he had absinthe. After dinner, at a fixed moment, came his coffee and cognac; then his tumbler of strong waters. It was all so regular, and so dull, that you had, when once you had remarked upon it, to go on watching it. It became a fascination. You began to understand that they lived by clockwork; hour to hour was struck by something to be done, eaten or prepared for eating, slept upon, walked in, taken off a peg, or hung up on one. The regularity of it absorbed you. You used, as a working hypothesis, the belief that these were not real people, but automata; and when you had to discard that by some unexpected flash or flicker you wondered how they could go on doing it and not go mad. And finally you judged that severe routine may as easily keep you from going mad as send you so.

I don't pretend to say—I never asked him—

whether observation on Hector's part preceded discovery; whether, that is, facts of these people's daily life slowly accumulated like a pile of kindling, and then, perhaps, broke into fire by their own pressure and mass; or whether he himself brought the burning glass and by the light of that revealed and fired the dreadful dry heap. I really don't know exactly how it was that the underlying, the recluded heart of the thing stood nakedly before his ingenuous, but quite candid, gaze. My own observation of the pair followed on his concernment with them. All I need say now is that on the evening arranged by the Fates I came down dressed for dinner and found him concerned—up to the neck.

II

ILLUMINATION

HECTOR was dressed before I was half-way through my bath. I know that because I heard him throw his boots down and then bang his door. On my way down-stairs to the hall where we used to assemble I saw him leaning against a pillar. He was scowling; but he couldn't help that—that was facial: otherwise he might have been saying his prayers or (which is the same thing with his sort) looking at a woman. His eyes were grey, and looked black at night. People— even women—thought him a black-eyed man. He was thin, sallow, elegant, and had jet-black hair. Not so good-looking as all that came to, he had a trustworthy face because it was essentially a simple one. You knew where you were with a face like that; you knew that it disguised nothing; you felt that there was nothing to disguise. Again, he had a caressing manner. I found him soothing— I knew a great many others did. Then he

24

had good teeth, and a singularly sweet smile.
It was that in particular which saved him
from the acute crisis frequently brought on
him by his want of tact. For tactlessness
he was without a peer. You would have
thought men and women centipedes from the
havoc Hector did among their toes. As for
his own treadings, he would have made a
faux pas on the last day. But his smile
saved him: that never failed. And he was
a lovable creature. If he made more enemies
than were good for any man, he turned them
all into friends—which was perhaps worse.
Bless him, anyhow, for a donkey, the most
sincere, irresistible, serious-minded, enthusiastic, impracticable donkey that ever brought
a stick about his ears.

But all this is a digression. He tempts
me to parentheses; but it is the fact that
he was looking at a woman. He and she
were conspicuous in a hall which even then
was three parts full of diners, moving about,
hailing each other, recounting the prowesses
of the day or the schemes for to-morrow.
Certainly I had not seen her before or I think
I must have remarked her. A tallish woman,

she was; pale, with a face like a star. That is poetry perhaps—it is, to be just to him, Hector's poetry—but like all poetry it is true. She had a starry face, a kind of divine, remote limpidity, as if she smiled in her own atmosphere, apart from the dust and heat of ours. She carried herself rarely, and though she was plainly dressed she had the air of jewels about her—especially in her hair. I mean that her head seemed to be lifting a coronet. Her hair was dark, lustrous and abundant, smooth over her brows, heavily looped and bunched behind. It was like a hood to her, thrown back to rest upon the nape and shoulders. I suppose that she really was tall, but being modestly formed she did not look her height. Her matronly air was seated in her eyes and lips. It was impossible to suppose her unmarried. You couldn't have thought that for a moment. She had no lines on her face; but I put her down for thirty-five. Malleson in his ardour said thirty, and turned out to be right. She was dressed that evening in black—black silk and lace—without any ornaments but a few rings. I noticed afterwards that she always dressed in black or white—so long, that is, as she remained at Gironeggio.

I had come down from my part of the house by the lift, which brought me out behind Malleson. The lady stood at the foot of the stairs at the other end of the hall. She was alone, but evidently waiting for a companion.

"Austrian," I said over Malleson's shoulder, and made him jump.

He shook me off in momentary irritation. "You would label the Venus of Milo," he said, and I replied that the Louvre had saved me the trouble, but that I would certainly have done it if necessary.

"Such women have no country," Hector said, as if to himself. I suggested the Pays du Tendre; but I don't think he heard me.

There were a great many people about, and she was not, I hope, aware of our unaffected interest in her. I trusted then, I am quite sure now, that we were not so conspicuous to her as she was to us. She had, anyhow, that peculiar possession of the well-bred, that power of ignoring what is disagreeable or uncomfortable—of ignoring it out of existence, you may say. She remained where she was,

with one hand upon the banister-rail, not so
much indifferent to the assemblage about her
as independent of it. I don't think she knew
that we were there—any of us. Her simplicity
was upon her like a panoply, so much so that
one was almost provoked by it, conscious of
a desire to try it, to find out whether it was
as shock-proof as it seemed. But after a
while it reacted upon me, and I felt that we
couldn't stop there forever.

"Come," I said. "We can't spy upon
her."

Hector murmured some inaudible thing.
By this time the diners had begun to flock
into the *salle à manger*, and I saw our common
friend Chevenix already at our table.

"Come along," I repeated. "Chevenix is
arranging his table-napkin. I see him at it."

"Wait," said Malleson. "Wait. Or go
if you like. I stay here. I can't come yet."

At that minute—the hall being nearly
emptied of its folk—a dark bulk loomed in
the passage beside the stairs which lead from
the ground-floor rooms; and then I heard
a peculiar sliding noise, as if one was dragging
a weight over the floor. The lady looked

quickly round, left her anchorage and stood facing the dining-room doors. This then was her companion: a darkly flushed, bearded man, square-shouldered, round-headed, dragging a foot, and moving out of the dark, as it seemed by main force. A wounded monster, a maimed Titan, haling himself along.

He had a stick in each clenched hand, and got along rather than walked. It must have been enormous labour—you could see the muscles grappling with the problem—you could see that each step, indeed, was a new problem; and yet his eyes were twinkling; he smiled into the lady's face: he, too, had patience, to cope with hers. I saw the meeting of eyes: his laughing to ask, hers not giving, but rather accepting. As he drew level with her she turned, and accommodating her pace to his, together they went into the dining-room. She was built for swiftness, but she curbed herself. I saw his square shoulders doggedly conquering the inches to the table, doggedly dragging that dead weight.

What more Malleson saw, or what he had seen, I can't tell you. He turned upon me a tragic look.

"Doom," he said. "A human sacrifice—
appointed to live, not to die. I feel sick at
the heart."

He looked as if he was charged with heavy
fate—as if all the burden of two unhappy
creatures whom he had never seen before in
his life had been piled on to his pair of slim
shoulders: but I knew him well. I made the
best of it, for his sake.

"It's bad," I admitted. "It's bad, but
it might be worse. Did you see her come
into the hall?"

He looked at me for a few seconds without
speaking. Then he nodded his head and
looked away. I waited. Presently he said—
it was as if I had compelled him—"She came
down-stairs." It is true, I had intended him
to tell me that, as I say, for his own sake.

"Come," I said; "we'll go and dine."
But he shook me off.

"Dine as you will. I can't. I shall go out
and walk about. I'll get something to eat
when I want it. I can't go in there. I don't
want to see them again just yet. I tell you I
can't afford it."

I didn't reason with him—why should I?

It would have been foolishness. So I left him and joined the exasperated Chevenix, a copper-headed, red-faced, very complacent friend, who was said to be easily the best-dressed man in Gironeggio.

I saw him with extended hand and fire in his blue eyes threatening the waiter. He had no fulmination to spare for me—at least, I think not.

"What the devil . . ." he was saying, but at the same moment his soup came to him, and did more than any excuses from me. He addressed himself to that. "It might be hotter," he said, "but it seems nourishing. Where's Malleson?"

I explained that Malleson wasn't dining. Chevenix looked momentarily concerned.

"What's up?" he asked. "Toothache? Telegrams? Can I do anything?"

"Nothing, Chevenix," I assured him, and looked about for the real cause of trouble.

They had a side-table and a diligent attendance. I guessed them immediately for persons of consequence, because the head-waiter had such a careful eye for them. Apart from that, they looked it. The man, with his square

bulk and hardy eyes, had the assured air of
the comfortably cushioned in this world, that
air of a corner-seat which the great, especially
the foreign great, are seldom without. An
English peer is very often apologetic. He
seems to say, "Excuse my greatness. I was
born to it—it's a thing that can't be helped."
The French aristocrat, on the other hand, is
frank about it. "I am somebody, and you are
canaille. True. But all that apart, how can I
serve you?" And as for the German—it is like
the rest of his system. It is the act of God.

I put these people down as Austrians, and
Chevenix, when I called his attention to them,
agreed.

"Austrian, right," he said. "You can
always tell. If ever you see Germans who
seem sorry about it, and anxious to be something else, they are Austrians. Very nice
people—except to each other. There, I happen to know, they are the deuce. I knew
a couple once—" But at that moment he
stopped. He stared—he grew red—he looked
the other way.

"Sorry," he said, then to me in a tragic
whisper, "Bad case."

I had seen what he had seen. The man by sheer muscular force had managed to drink out of a wine-glass. He had collected, concentrated, his will-power upon it, grappled with it, rocked it to and fro in mighty conflict, drained it, and set it down. It gave you much the same effect as you would get at a circus from an elephant lighting a cigar—that of enormous concentration, of incredible difficulties overcome by strength. It was a question of a few seconds only; yet I had seen the gathering of the forces for attack, the clutching hand, the putting forth of all his strength—and the futility of effort. It affected me very much. I felt it tragic and horrible at once.

It set Chevenix moralizing at random. "That's bad, you know, when you get it like that. Uses up your reserves, what? And all for a drink! All for love and the world well lost, eh? Oh, quite so, quite so! But for a glass of claret!" He mused, and I had lost the thread of his discourse when he broke out again. "I knew a man—married to a jolly pretty woman, too—who had no feet at all. Accident, you know. Volcano

or something. Found himself in lava—that
sort of thing. Pegs he had—two pegs. No
feet. He used to go dotting about with two
sticks. You might have been following your
own dressing-table, I assure you. . . . A
pretty woman, too. Yet he seemed to give
satisfaction. She never looked at anybody
else—so far as *I* know."

"You mean that she didn't look at you,
I suppose?" I ventured.

"Right," said Chevenix. "That's just
what I do mean."

"Now, with our friend over there," he
continued, when he had helped himself to
ice-pudding, "I should say that *she* was
considerably bored. Shouldn't you? She's
your still-water sort—*that* you can see. *She*
never told her love. Not she. Sooner die.
Bless you, I know that kind. Damask cheek,
what? I suppose, you know, that it took
her unawares. And him, too. A thief in
the night. Oh, it's pretty thick, a thing of
that sort. And—I say!" He suddenly fixed
me with a very open and alert pair of eyes.
"I say, what's the matter with Malleson,
anyhow?"

I must say that Bill Chevenix, with the manners of a first-class ass, has a far-reaching intelligence. Here, however, he rather divined than inferred.

I said, "Malleson has seen them."

"And it has knocked him out? Well, he's a sensitive plant. But Broderode's all right."

I jumped. "What!" I said. "You know them, then?"

He grew explanatory. "My dear man, I know their names—that's as far as I am prepared to go at present. He is a Baron Eugene von Broderode—and she is his Baroness."

"Then you've seen them before?"

Chevenix tossed his head. "Seen them before? I should hope so. When did you ever know me *not* see a pretty woman before? You imagine a vain thing."

I said that she was more than a pretty woman, and he allowed it. I said that she was a beautiful woman, by which I largely mean a woman made beautiful by a beautiful nature. A kind of lamp, illuminated from within. I judged that she was not a happy woman and didn't see how she could expect to be; but I allowed a great deal for use-

and-wont, and wasn't prepared to be as shocked as the too susceptible Hector had been. I considered that she was chiefly bored, but I admit that I had not gone deeply into her case. Perhaps you need imagination to do that. I don't think I have much of it. I did notice, however, that they were a silent couple, speaking only upon commonplaces; I noticed also that such talk as there was came from him. She answered, but carelessly, as if such prattle was not worth notice. Then again there was this. He sought her attention and occasionally compelled it. She looked at him when she had to, but not unless he made her. Letters and a newspaper or two were brought to them by the ever-watchful head-waiter. She opened his for him, as the poor fellow was making a dreadful mess of it. Her own occupied her for the rest of the meal. She ate hardly anything; but he, on the contrary, did himself extremely well, and wrestled for his wine with a zeal worthy of a better cause. To see him at that was to witness an enthralling spectacle. A battle on a large scale—masses engaged—no quarter —and all for a glass of claret!

After dinner we took our coffee in the
Lounge with a cosmopolitan Dutchman from
The Hague, who knew everybody. Eugene
von Broderode was our man's name, he agreed.
She was a Pole, he believed. His family,
of course, was from the Low Countries; he
bore an historical name; but he was of a
younger branch of it long settled in Galicia.
A very accomplished man, great traveller,
spoke English as well as we did; had been
in diplomacy, and was so when our friend
saw most of him—in Rome that had been,
in '86-'88. We saw how it was with him?
Here Chevenix nodded sagely and looked
concerned. Never be surprised at such things,
said our friend. His manner of life had been
—here he shrugged up into the air—absurd
—up to the hilt. He went into life, as you
can find it when you want it, with the zest
of a young giant. It had been one long series
of pursuits. And in at the death every time.
He shrugged his chorus to the strokes of
Doom. "He got out by marriage—as you
see. Just in time, as it seemed. She was
a girl of eighteen—out of a convent school.
It was twelve or more years ago. Nearer

fourteen, I should say. She didn't make a
fuss—either from pure ignorance or because
they never do. For they don't, you know.
If once they began that, God knows where
they would end—" There he paused and
stroked the ash off his cigar against the
match-box. He rolled the glowing stump
about in his ·fingers; and then said slowly
and with great distinctness, "And I think
he would be a bad friend to a woman who
taught her that her lot might be very much
better than it is—in every case."

We had no commentary to offer upon
this dictum; but I thought of my grave-eyed
friend pacing the shores of the lake.

Meantime I had been observing the pair
upon whose nature and lot Van Riiver had
been moralizing. They sat apart in a recess
by the staircase, she with her needles and
silk, he with his cigar. I admired the play
of her beautiful hands, but still more her extraordinary patience. At the allotted moment came the coffee equipage and the old
brandy. She busied herself with that, serving
him but not herself, and then resumed her
netting. He, apparently at ease, literally

drank at his cigar, and inhaled the last pint
of joy from it. Yet you could see that he
kept a watchful eye for his grim, unsleeping
enemy, and gave not one inch of ground.
If his paper slipped from his knee he called
up his forces to recover it. It came up flut-
tering like a rag in a gale—but it came.
She did not help him: one saw that he would
not allow that. By incredible efforts he
accomplished what was needful with the
appearance of ease. I warmed to him for
his courage and audacity; and when he began to play patience, and at every shift of
a card had to risk battle and rout—and
nearly always triumphed—horrible as the
flickering business was to watch, I felt that
I could have been proud either of his friendship or his enmity. He was no shirker. He
faced the foe. There was no faltering. The
foe would pin him at last; but he would
go to his death with the flag flying.

He was a strong man armed, with his
handsome, galliard, shining face. He had
kind, blue, humorous eyes, eyes which were
kind even in the trap's teeth, and did not
cease their laughing scrutiny. You couldn't

catch him out anywhere. He was ready for
you at all points. He seemed to me abound-
ingly clever and capable, so thoroughly
awake as he was to a delicate situation. Occasionally, I went so far as to judge, he was
foolhardy in his gallantry; he took risks
which were heavy. But I thought I could
hear his apology. "See," he might well be
saying, "see how it is that, with this ghastly
shackling upon me, I still hold this lovely
creature at a nod. There's no chain; there's
nothing but a confident look." That was
true; there was no appeal. "I put it to you.
You took me; here I am as you see me. Well,
what are we to make of it, you and I?" I
am not saying that there is no other side to
this brave shield of his. I am saying that
this was gallantry.

Chevenix, rendered grave by Van Riiver's
reminiscences, had been blinking his light
eyelashes over them. Then he said that he
remembered a murder case where the defence
was something like this. The accused said
that he had sat opposite the murdered woman
for something like twenty years without
speaking. It had become a habit. They

had not quarrelled, but they had nothing
to say; so they didn't speak. Then, one
evening, it struck him like a fire-ball from
heaven, "Lord of Life and Death, I shall
have to sit opposite this woman for twenty
years more perhaps—and neither of us has
a word to say. It is not to be borne." He
yielded to the impulse—and he killed her.

Van Riiver chuckled. "Did they allow
the plea?"

"They did not," said Chevenix.

"They hanged him?"

"They did."

Van Riiver said, "Perhaps it was well.
And yet it's as likely a form of madness as
any other that leads to sudden violence."

"Mind you," said Chevenix, "the thought
might drive anybody mad. What! All
silent and all damned!"

"Yes," said Van Riiver, getting up. "But
no woman would have had the thought for
a moment. It would have seemed quite in
the order of things."

Thereupon he left us and crossed the room
to greet our pair. Baron von Broderode
gaily held out his left hand. The Baroness

smiled up at him from her work, but offered
no more formal greeting. Van Riiver bowed
deeply to her, and began to talk. The Baron
laughed and joked, but never ceased for one
moment his running battle. Every card
that he moved flickered terribly in his hand.

We watched them for a while. Then Chevenix said, "Good old Hector. He should
have been here. He'd have been interested.
Come and play French pills. I'll take you
on."

III

IMPLICATION

WE saw nothing of Hector that night, but
before it was ended our Dutch acquaintance
had presented Chevenix and me formally
to the Baron and his fair wife. That was
exciting, as actual contact must always be,
where the person touched has been the ob-
ject of more or less intense speculation. He
bristles at every point with the darts of your
surmises. I found him, as I had expected,
most affable; he spoke fluent, idiomatic
English—occasionally at fault. He rose to
greet us—I saw his brow break into beads
of sweat as he did it: but do it he would and
did. He said that he was delighted to see
us, and I really thought that he was. She
contented herself with bending her beautiful head—an act like that of a princess
bowing from a carriage—but by and by
she slid into the conversation, and towards
the end she could laugh and be at ease with
my engaging, red-headed friend, who, with

a casual manner, always succeeded in getting
interest, because he always gave it.

I forget what we all talked about—anything or nothing, as people do in hotels; but
I do remember that Chevenix brought in
the absent Hector. "A very serious young
man," he told the Baroness. "Malleson,"
he said, "is a man who thinks that he was
born to put the world to rights. O cursèd
spite! I beg your pardon—not at all. He
doesn't mind doing it in the least; but it
weighs upon him all the same. He feels the
responsibility. The time is slipping by, you
see. He thinks us all very frivolous." She
was prepared for his examples; she could
see that he was seething with anecdote—
but it was her husband who spoke. I didn't
think he had been listening.

"How is he getting on—your friend?" he
asked, deeply appreciative of the nature of
the man thus lightly etched in.

Chevenix tossed his head. "He wrestles
with it, sir. He's out and about now, seeing
that the lake does its duty. 'Roll on, thou
deep and dark blue ocean, roll'—which it
does not fail to do, with Malleson's encour-

agement. Do you read Byron?" With that
he turned to the lady. She confessed to
having read the poet—when she was a girl.

"There's nothing Byronic about Hector,"
Chevenix told her, "except his pre-occupa-
tion with eternity. Hector's a very religious
man. He'll end up a Catholic, I don't
doubt—and then he'll be all right. The
Church, you see, will take his responsibilities
from him. Byron would have done the same,
if he'd had time."

The Baron agreed. "You are right, Mr.
Chevenix," he said. "Voltaire was a pose
with Byron. He wore him like plate armour.
He scorned himself, that young man, and
took pains to be scornful of the world in order
to let himself down, as you say. There never
was any man of his ability and force who got
less out of this world than your Lord Byron."
Here he drank prodigiously of his cigar.

"There," said Chevenix to me as we
watched him heave out of sight, trailing his
feet into the dusk of the passage, "there
goes a man who will squeeze the last drops
out of life." The implication of this heedless
remark struck me all of a heap, as the com-

panion of the ruthless Titan turned her head, and showed us her tragic profile. From what lives was he not squeezing the last drops? I was able to appreciate Hector's concern, though, unlike Hector, I did not propose to take any steps.

Van Riiver chuckled grimly. "Oh, he will squeeze life with anybody. He has always done that."

"Did you notice," Chevenix said, after a moment of amused reflection, "how he drank his cigar?"

"That was how he drank—everything," Van Riiver said. "He went over them like a hot wind."

"Them?" said Chevenix, with a lift of the eyebrow. Van Riiver nodded.

"Them," he said. "And now he's footing the bill."

I said that he did it like a man. Van Riiver shrugged.

"He gets a lot of help, you know," he said.

I thought of that pale and tragic profile, turned sideways as if looking for help. I was glad that Hector had not been there—for what can you do?

In the morning Chevenix went his ways,
entrenched in portmanteaux and kit-bags.
I saw him to the station on his way to Rome.
"Look after Hector," were his parting words.
"He'll want it. There's divine simplicity
pealing in that lady's eyes. He'll hear it as
you and I hear the dinner-gong."

"I know he's very susceptible," I said.
"Put it down to youth. And women are
to be fallen in love with."

"Right," said Chevenix. "The Catholics
knew what they were about."

"I'm sure of it," said I. "Bless you, she's
older then Hector."

"She's a dangerous age. I'll tell you a
good thing I read somewhere. I don't know
who said it, but I daresay you do. 'After
forty a woman gets bored with virtue and a
man with honesty.'"

"Sydney Smith said that," I told him.
"But be just to our friends. Neither of
them is forty yet."

"She's words to that effect," said Chevenix, "and as for him, the devil of it is
that he'll never get tired of honesty. If he did
he'd be harmless. I knew a man once—

We're off. I leave it at that. So long."
He waved his hand, and went out, veiled
in anecdote to the last.

I found Hector at his coffee in the sun.
He looked sedate, pre-occupied, and saluted
me remotely. He did not seem inclined to
discuss his agitation of overnight, and it
wasn't for me to begin upon it. I asked him
if he had any plans for the day: he said,
none. I asked him had he thought of our
movements? He said he had not. I was by
this time somewhat ruffled and inclined to
damn his eyes at a venture.

I said, "We should have been glad of
your company last night, and I think that
you would have been glad of ours. Van
Riiver was very interesting."

"He can be, I know," Hector said. "He's
a wicked old sinner, but all the better company for that."

"Yes," I said, "and he knows everyone.
That's useful sometimes."

I think he began to have an inkling. He
shot me a moment's glance, then deliber-
ately drank before he answered.

"Very useful. Did he find some acquaintance last night?"

"He did," I said, "and we made some."

Hector's sallow skin burned—a sort of
brick-red suffused him.

"The von Broderodes are friends of his.
We were presented, Chevenix and I."

Hector's hand shook as he filled a pipe.
He was very agitated.

"My dear chap—" he began, then he
started and stopped.

"Look here, Hector," I said, "we'll get
out of this place as soon as you please—"
He began to fume.

"You may do as you like. I have no power
to stop you. I had better tell you at once
that I have no intention of going, and that
I don't recognize any right in the world—"

I laughed at him; a stupid thing to do.
"You wouldn't recognize it if you saw it
hard upon your nose," I said. "And there
is no right in the matter, if you come to that.
But I have rights of my own all the same,
just as you may have; and if you believe it
your right to languish over a married woman,
I am sure it is mine to avoid the spectacle.

4

I shall go to Milan and make preparations.
You'll pick me up when you want me."

"My dear fellow," said Hector quietly
and with immense gravity, "I never wanted
you more than I do now. You are the best
friend I have in the world—and God knows
I want a friend."

He touched me. I felt sorry for him. He
was an ass, but he was such a generous ass.
Besides that, I couldn't resist him. I ought
to have known better, and I did; but he had
me on my weak side. So instead of scoffing
at him, as I should have done, I took him
for a walk and had it out of him.

He had fallen in love with this lady, instantly and plumply in love—but in the
modest, reverential way which becomes a
young man of his sort. After all, young men
are at their best when they are in love, and
before there is any question of the hunter's
instinct being aroused. He talked about
her as he might have talked about his mother,
if he had had one alive; half mother, half
goddess, he made her out. He had spent
the night on the mountain side, he told me,
and had hardly known it was night before

the dawn came. "I felt," he said, "that the moment of a lifetime was come upon me. I felt the call—for I must tell you what I suppose you haven't known, that our eyes met there in the hall across all those babbling idiots. They did, you know. Whatever may come of it—and God knows what that may be—we are not the same people. You can't explain these things, you can't account for them. It's as if we had invisible tentacles streaming out of us, waving, spearing into the air. These never touch but what is sympathetic: they curl and writhe and avoid all else. But by the thrill that ran all through me, and by the divine illumination of her face at that moment, I swear to you that she and I touched each other. The thing's done and can't be undone."

I took it lightly, though with heavy foreboding. "All right," I said, "it's done then. But this is a cut-and-dried world, after all, and there's a Baron of experience in the way. No tentacles streaming out of Baron Eugene."

"Is his name Eugene?" Hector asked me with great interest.

"So Van Riiver tells me," I answered. "Why not?"

"Oh, no reason whatever. Only it's odd, because I believe that her name is Eugenia."

"But it isn't," I said. "I happened to see her name on an envelope. It is Helena. I hope yours isn't going to be Paris."

He was muttering to himself. "I thought it was Eugenia. It *is* Eugenia so far as I am concerned."

I said rather brutally, "She must be thirty at least. She's been married twelve years, and Van Riiver says that she was a girl when he married her."

He wasn't listening to me. I heard him say "Eugenia" once or twice softly to himself. He was very far gone.

I offered to introduce him, but he said that wasn't necessary. I told him that she wouldn't drop her handkerchief for him, not being that kind. He said that I didn't understand these things. When I offered to retail him some more of the Dutchman's gossip, he cut me off short. "I'm sure you mean well, you are the best friend I have. But, you see, you and I are at cross-purposes

over this. You think that I am going to
make love to her, and very reasonably want
to head me off. Well, I am not. You don't
make what already exists. I have made all
the love I intend to make her. The thing
is done."

"Well, what do you intend to do next?"
I asked him.

He said he didn't know. He should see
her every day. That was all he could be
sure of at present. I left it at that.

As it fell out, Van Riiver caught us that
afternoon as we returned from a long walk,
and before he knew where he was Hector
was presented to his Eugenia. He was
handsomely confused, she serenely uncon-
scious of waving tentacles, to all appearance.
The Baron was cordial and rose up on his
two sticks like the unwearied Titan he was.
First he lifted his hat with a flourish which
must have cost him something; then he held
out his hand. "I am very glad to meet Mr.
Malleson. The more so because I have his
name by heart. It must have been a relation
of yours who was a friend of mine long ago.

He was in diplomacy, and so also I. First in Madrid—that was in '90; and then in Petersburg. But he is dead—and I am sorry."

That was what he said, with great ease and friendly interest. Hector heard him in a stare which showed me that he himself was not at all interested. He recovered himself just in time to avoid an awkwardness.

"Ah, yes," he said, "you mean my uncle Bellasys. Yes, he is dead. He went to Teheran on a mission, and died out there."

"He was a good fellow," said the Baron, warming to his reminiscences—"a good fellow. What you call a cool cucumber. I will tell you a tale of your Uncle Bellasys. It was at Nice, in the earthquake. He was shaving at his window, when, all in a moment, he sees a factory chimney down in the town break off short like a carrot and fall. At the same moment all the walls of the room begin to sway about like seaweed in the tide. The people all run out into the garden in their nightgowns—the trees begin to crack and the chimneys to tumble. But your Uncle Bellasys—he goes on shaving." Hector taking it modestly—as any one would take praises of his uncle—the Baron turned glowing to Van Riiver. "Hey, Van Riiver, what do you say? You knew Bellasys Malleson—hey? He was a cool cucumber."

I enjoyed the cool cucumber, Van Riiver applauded the uncle, and we all became very friendly. Hector sat by his Eugenia— I mean, of course, the Baroness Helena— and received tea from her. I didn't observe much intercourse between them, though no doubt the tentacles were at work. The Baron, who was in great form, never left them alone for long together; but I was interested to observe that he rarely addressed his wife. It was Hector whom he called in to the general conversation.

I had a few words with her, and judged that she was of a cold temperament. If she had ever suffered, that was all over. She had been broken in, had found her line of least resistance and, like a wise woman, stuck to it. All this comforted me. I doubted whether Hector would get her off the track, or be tempted off it himself. There were possibilities—there always are possibilities

where a man is in earnest and a woman
bored. But I judged by her eyes, which were
direct, grey, and very cool. You could see
the thought concentrating in them before
she spoke. The pupils palpitated, enlarged
and contracted like sea-anemones. Finally
she volunteered a fact which in my opinion
settled it. She had a child—in Vienna—a
girl. I was interested, and allowed myself
to appear so.

"You should have brought her to Gironeggio," I said. "How she would have liked
these mountains!"

"Yes, but it was not possible," she answered. "She has her tutors and govern-
esses. She is very ambitious. And she knows
the mountains very well. Every year she
is in the Tyrol."

"She is ambitious! It is early days to
encourage ambition," I suggested.

"She is ten," said the Baroness with a
steady look.

And so on, and so on! I don't think that
she was interested in me, and don't wonder
either. She was a lovely woman, but not my
kind. I don't like cold women, and have

no use whatever for women who don't like me. A few more general remarks found me at the end of my tether. I excused myself in the usual manner—letters to write—and went off for a bath, leaving Malleson with his lady.

After dinner he was with them again.

IV

INTENTION

I SHALL summarize rapidly a week's work, and come to a curious episode which marks a definite stage in my history. It was a week in which I had to see my ingenuous friend get enmeshed in what he was pleased to call the Baroness' tentacles, though, to do the fair lady justice, she made no visible exertions toward it. Indeed, if tentacles there were, they were Baron Eugene's, which could not have enough of poor Hector's. He seemed to have no objections at all to his wife obtaining a *cavalier servant*. The marvel was that she hadn't half a dozen to do the cushion-carrying, chair-moving, bell-ringing which he himself, poor chap, was prevented from doing. Malleson was absorbed in the tender business, and had plenty of urbanity to spare for the Baron. So they made a pleasant little party of three.

He got very little out of it but the consciousness of devoted attentions. He was

58

hardly ever alone with her, hardly ever exchanged—tentacles apart—half-a-dozen words
with her which the Baron didn't hear: none,
I am certain, which the Baron was not intended to hear. Nor were there any of those
conscious glances to be intercepted, which
really tell a man more of the state of a case
than all the words of a *tête-à-tête* put together. Hector, who had ordinarily about
as much tact as a tortoise, seemed to have
understood for once with whom he was deal-
ing. Helena was divinely simple, as he had
said, and therefore divinely guarded. An
angel with a sword stood upon her quiet
brows. Hector must have seen him there,
and respected the blazoned cross on his
shield. But I know that he was deeply in
love with her, because he was so happy.

He was at that stage of love when the
consciousness of love itself is a triumph. It
is the elated feeling which a poet has when
he has written a poem, which a hen has when
she has laid an egg. You go clucking about;
you lift your feet up; your head is in the
stars. Such a spectacle is always exhilarat-
ing—I speak for myself, who am never bored

with an ardent lover. Hector was one. He asked nothing, expected nothing and got nothing. And as he too was innocent, it never occurred to him, at this stage of affairs, to consider curiously, to let his imagination range over the lives of these two ill-accorded beings—this stricken hulk which had so little left him of mannishness but mannish appetite, and this late-flowering, bound and nobly reticent lady. Although his interest in Helena had been heightened, deepened, inflamed by her hard fate, remember that it had been there before. Her beauty had inspired it— and it was her beauty which washed out that temporary fever of interest, and remained as a holy and purely delightful possession of his. I speak of the first week of his admitted passion for Helena. What happened after that, while I was away, I shall have to report before I have done with this chapter of events.

My own intercourse with the von Broderodes was casual and intermittent. We saluted each other when we met. The Baron used to wave his hand to me across the dining-room; once or twice a look passed between us

which, on his side at least, was one of intelligence to impart. He seemed to be telling
me that he knew all about it. And I'll go
bail that he did. He was so very much on
the spot, as Chevenix would have said. His
was the whip hand, you see. He drove on
the snaffle, and she had a tender mouth. He
knew all about that; and I thought that he
wished *me* to know that he did. More than
once, certainly, I saw his watchful blue eyes
fixed upon me—to see how I was taking
Hector's devotion and her calm acceptance
of it. It seems absurd—but once I am morally
certain that he winked. It was when Hector
was holding silk for her to wind. To be sure,
a man does not look at his best when he is at
that duty, and assuredly, if he is not a lover,
he is a fool, according to Baron von Broderode.

One day—it was in the garden and after
tea—it so happened that I found myself
walking with the Baroness. I am not sure
that she did not contrive it. Hector was held
in talk by the Baron, and she, with what was
practically an invitation, got up and began
to walk the grass. I followed her.

She began to question me about Hector's
people—with really very little preface. She
said that she liked him very much; she felt
sure that he must be "noble," because he
was so sincere, and took so much for granted.
I told her that he was what she would call
noble, but pointed out that in Britain we had
both nobility and rank. Hector's rank, I
said, was not very great—not so great as her
own—but his nobility was as fine as you please.
Sir Roderick, I told her, was a kind of petty
king in his own country.

She pondered this. What did I mean,
exactly? I told her that there were some three
or four thousand people who would profess it
their duty to shed their blood for Sir Roderick
Malleson; and that when Sir Roderick died,
Hector would be Sir Hector, and might look
for the same devotion.

She said that that was like Hungary, and
that her own country had been like that too,
once upon a time.

I said, "You are a Pole, Baroness?"

"Yes," she said, "I am a Pole, but there is
no Poland now."

She returned to the Mallesons. Hector had

brothers, she had been told. Did I know
them? I told her that I knew them all.
Hector was the eldest. Then there were
Nigel, a sailor, Spenser, a priest, Wynyard
and Pierpoint, who were twins, and Patrick.
There were no daughters.

Were they much alike? she wanted to
know. I told her that physically they were
divided into camps. Hector, Nigel the sailor,
and Patrick, who was at Oxford, were all
dark, like their mother, who had been a dark,
slim, grey-eyed woman. The middle three
favoured the father, tall and broad-shouldered,
fair-haired young men. I told her that these
three had been a great trio in their day.

She bent her brows, "But their day is
not over?"

I told her, no indeed. But Spenser, who
had been brought up by the Jesuits, was now
a priest and in China; and as for the twins,
they had separated widely as they had grown
up. Pierpoint was a soldier, and Wynyard a
mighty hunter. Fine young men both, but
very unlike in character.

She absorbed my information. "Tell me
more about them," she said very simply. I

gave her thumb-nail sketches of Pierpoint's gallant ways, and of Wynyard, the lean and silent. Then I threw her off a portrait of the old chief himself. "You would like him," I assured her. "He is the finest and the youngest of them all. His faith never fails him."

"His faith in what?" she asked.

"In himself," I said. "He is in his way a king of men. Indeed, he is actually that. There was the case of a man in his country who got a summons for debt. He brought it up to the chief to know what he ought to do about it. I assure you that the King's writ runs there on sufferance."

She wasn't good at little jokes. She took that quite sedately. "But your friend, Mr. Hector—" she began again—"he is the heir, as you say. Do they—has he got authority— I don't know how to put it, but I suppose he would have to exercise some sort of authority in such a house?"

"He hasn't been called upon for any as yet," I said, smiling, "but I think that he could be trusted. There has been no mutiny so far."

She trembled upon her next question. "His father—are they good friends?"

I didn't know where she was leading me—
I evaded. "Oh, well, you know, he's the heir,
and of course there are difficulties—but on
the whole I don't think they do so badly."
I wasn't going to tell her everything—for instance, that Sir Roderick was only fond of
Hector when he wasn't there. The truth, of
course, was that they were too much alike
ever to get on.

Presently she began again—and I began to
see where I was. "Mr. Malleson has invited
us to Inveroran," she said, "and I think my
husband would like to go. But I feel that it is
rather a long journey for him. Nothing is
decided."

"I am sure you would like Inveroran," I
told her. "The place is really magnificent—
fourteenth century, most of it; and as for
the scenery—! No doubt, after your Car-
pathians, your Dolomites and your Alps, you
would be exacting in that matter; but you
must remember that in Scotland they have
the sea as a foreground."

She smiled rather bleakly. "I don't think
I am exacting," she said. Poor dear! I
should think she wasn't.

5

By that time we were close to the others, and our conversation died out.

This was how the affair stood when I went away and left Hector behind me. I really wanted to do some work in Lombardy; I was no good to him where I was, and with matters in that trim; moreover, I admit, I judged that all was well. I trusted in her discretion as much as in his simplicity—but it seems that while you can push simplicity to the edge of a precipice you must not always expect it to drop meekly off into the inane. I hadn't taken the Baron's bravado into account—and perhaps he hadn't either, himself. To put it quite shortly, after ten days' absence I had a telegram from Hector, asking me to meet him in Milan without fail.

I hate the place, and was being cut off just when my work was beginning to arrange itself — was doing a map of Roman Lombardy— but of course I went.

I found him pacing the hall of the hotel, jumping from lozenge to lozenge of the chequered pavement, in a pair of red morocco slippers. His hands behind his back, his head bent, his brows knitted, he seemed to be concentrated upon his ridiculous exercise. He looked like a young crane learning his father's daily antics. It was some time before he saw me watching him, and when he did, he stood where he was, balancing on one foot (exactly covering a black lozenge) and in his turn looked at me.

"Hulloa," I said— we had the place practically to ourselves. There was a page-boy asleep in a corner, his arms on the desk.

I got a rocking-chair and sat in it. I lit a cigarette. "Well?" I said. "What is it? A crisis?"

He hovered about me. "Yes," he said. "I don't know what to do next."

I strangled a guffaw at birth. "You must tell me first what you have done last. I suppose you have made love to her?"

He shook this away, as if it were water in his ear. "Don't talk rot, please. I haven't come to this beastly town, or pulled you into it, to talk about love-making. This is a matter of life and death."

"Whose life, my dear?" I said. "Whose death?"

"Her life," he told me then, "and anybody's death you please."

This annoyed me. "I wish you wouldn't talk minor poetry, Hector," I said. "Now look here. I must get you along. You have either said something that you ought not to have said or——"

"She knows, of course, that I love her. But that's an old story," said Hector. "I suppose she knew that the first evening."

"By wireless," I said. "By your tentacles —and hers, of course."

He nodded. "That's it. Yes, of course. But she knows it explicitly now. I told her."

"Oh, you did, did you? Well, what did she say?"

He became inspired. "Such women have no need to speak. She looked at me. I read every word she said. I accepted every command she laid upon me. There was nothing to do. I had said to her, 'You know that I love you. You know that I would die for you.' I read her answer. 'Yes, I know it. But to die for me would be too easy. I ask you to live for me.'"

I held my tongue from handling this flip-
pantly. Poor fellow, it was serious enough
this time. Presently I said that I considered
her answer a good one. "If you have read
her message rightly—and I expect you have
—you can only obey. But there's more to
come."

"There is," he said. "I tell you plainly,
I don't know what to do."

He became very much agitated. He took
a quick turn over the hall; and when he came
back he seemed panic-stricken. He came to
me all alight with the truth. His eyes were
like fires—fires in daylight—for he had no
colour.

"I must tell you," he said, breathing short.
"The man's a ghoul."

I had nothing to say. I waited. But I
remembered what Van Riiver had said, on
the night of our first acquaintance with the
pair, about squeezing the last drops out of life.

"He lives on her. He fastens himself.
Day by day. Andromeda white at the stake—
enfolded—day by day."

I kept my eyes upon him. With the eyes
only I inquired of his trouble.

He answered my unvoiced question. "Yes, he does. She is his, body and blood. Seven years of it—seven years—" Incoherence followed, which I don't attempt to put down.

He had fought with it for nearly a week. I'll undertake to maintain that he fought desperately, that it was a tooth-and-nail business. But it beat him, and changed everything. The affair would, but for that, have run a normal course. He would have adored her near and far for a season; but with the fair one in Austria and the swain in Scotland or parts adjacent, that season would not have been a long one. But now there was something added. The imagination was inflamed beyond quenching. The first momentary fire—when he saw the man come dragging himself down the passage in pursuit —had been a flicker. His native wholesomeness had put that out. Not so now. He knew the facts.

I did what I could for him, all that an older and cooler head can do for a man in such a state. But he fought me all along the line.

I said, "You have done a fatal thing. You have looked where you ought not——"

"It's not true," he said hotly. "He took me in—to show me a photograph."

"Very well, I'll admit it," I told him, "but still I say that you should have refused to consider. That, believe me, is the only possible course. That's the way of sanity. Don't ask me how people feel about these things. We've agreed to put a sanctity about life. What is a sanctity but a hedge? Woe to him who peers through. Very properly he gets the worst of it. Now here, you can do nothing—except go away. You've done that—and I hope you'll stick to it."

He was jumping about—all around me. "I don't know what I shall do yet. I know that I must do something."

"What on earth—" I began to say.

He said, "There are plenty of things that I might do. I think she knows it."

"She may very well fear the only thing that you could do," I told him.

He simply laughed at me: a mirthless laugh. "Oh, you fool," he said. "I don't want to do anything to her. Do you think I can't be trusted? You ought to know me by this time."

"Then, what *do* you want with her?" I asked him.

"I want her to be free," he said. "As free as the wind. You may say what you please about your sanctified hedges; but surely you see that every soul is responsible to itself. The hedge is there—from birth. It is not I who violate it. God help her, that was done long ago."

We lunched, and I got some more positive information out of him. The von Broderodes had left Gironeggio. *He* had gone to Galicia and was going on from there to Petersburg; thence to Moscow, where he had many friends and would stay for a month at least. He had his man with him, and the Italian woman, Teresa Visconti, without whom he never travelled a yard. *She* was to be in Vienna with the child. In the autumn they were all coming to Inveroran. The Baron intended to shoot, it seems.

In this state of affairs, what did Hector intend to do? He said that he should go home, he thought. She was happy where she was—which was all he seemed to care

about. He should certainly not go to Vienna.
She wouldn't like it—nor would he. Yes, he
intended to write to her. He had done so
already, but she hadn't answered him yet.
He didn't care if she did—much.

His passion had left him. He was depressed
and despondent.

I said, "I hope you mean to have me at
Inveroran. Your friends interest me very
much. I expect to see some fine shooting
from the Baron."

He drearily agreed with me. "I imagine
that he has shot most things shootable in his
day," he said. "I don't suppose he has
missed much."

"You are not in the mood to do him justice,"
I said. "Personally, I admire him. He's
putting up a great fight for it. You'll see,
he'll go down with his colours nailed to the
mast."

Hector turned rather green, and shut his
eyes. "We won't talk about him just now,"
he said; and then, "Damn him—he's a
ghoul."

V

INVERORAN

THE famous prayer, "Bless, we beseech Thee, O Lord, Great and Lesser Cumbrae, and the adjacent islands of Great Britain and Ireland," may well have been put up at Inveroran, where, as I happen to know, the King of England was looked upon as a neighbouring monarch. It was Sir Roderick's factor who remarked to me, on the occasion of a royal visit, when, after a Highland gathering, his Majesty drove off, accompanied by his host, "They'll be glad to be by themselves, no doubt." I must say that I like that sort of thing. Race interests me more than anything in the world; and up there you get it pure and strong. You feel a very long way from England at Inveroran.

The Castle stands finely on the rising ground above the bay, which has so narrow an entrance that it has all the appearance of an inland · water. Below the gates of the policies the little white town begins, and straggles down

to the quay and harbour. A steamer from
Glasgow puts in twice a week in the summer,
once a week in the winter, and when south-
westerly winds are blowing very often not
that. The moors stretch out in a demi-lune
on either side of you; and then over the
first ridge you come to the deer forest. They
say that you would hardly ride out of Malleson
land in a day if you chose to go north-east.
Personally, I have never tried. I am no
sportsman myself, and have no need to pretend
to be. It used to be one of the minor afflic-
tions of poor Hector's life-days that, next in
succession as he was, he was an extremely
bad performer with the rifle, while his younger
brothers were of the best. Wynyard, especially, was a crack shot.

They were all there for the shooting that
year, except Nigel the sailor, who was at
Malta, and Spenser the priest, still a missionary and martyr-elect in China. Wynyard
was there, as always, and in first-rate form,
and Pierpoint, the splendid young man, whom
some of us called George IV, because he had
the flushed and triumphant look of Lawrence's
portrait of the youthful monarch, and some

the Apollo Belvedere; and young Patrick,
too, a cool hand—or, as von Broderode would
say, a cool cucumber. I told him that joke
before the visitors came, and it was the aim
of his soul to make him say it. As a matter
of fact, the young ass said it himself before
the Baron had been in the place an hour,
and the Baron spotted it instantly as a wrong
idiom. He turned it very cleverly on Pat:
"What you call a cool cucumber," he used to
say to him, fixing him with his galliard blue
eye. That is only one of a thousand instances
when von Broderode turned a retreat into
a victory. How the man had time, where he
found zest for such little affairs, was a marvel
to me.

There were the usual sort of people there
to meet them. Some off-hand girls, very
sketchily dressed, rather cynical and extremely
wiry; their mothers or not, as the case might
be—there's no rule; a couple of colonels
who shot all day and played bridge all night.
One of them made money at it—and "By
Gad, I want it," he told me, and I believed
him. Then there were Lord Mark, who is a
Malleson uncle by the mother's side, and his

wife, American and rather stodgy. There were others, but they don't matter—youth from Oxford, speechless to the likes of me, but very eloquent at side-tables. And that's all.

I was there before the von Broderodes came, when, in fact, there was daily and gay speculation about them. To Patrick he was the "German Johnny" or "Old Two-Sticks" —which made Sir Roderick fume and scowl. Checked there, Pat turned him into Sir Leoline, the Baron rich, which was safe, since his father knew not the bard, but had horrid implications as to what he had or had not in his company, very useful against Hector on occasion. Sir Roderick didn't mind what was said so long as it was admitted that the von Broderodes were not German. He hated the Germans and thought that they intended the destruction of our realms, though not, of course, that they would succeed. To him it was very important that the Baron was Austrian—"Old friends of ours, the Austrians —a fine people, sir." He thought to call your prospective guest Old Two-Sticks was offensive—"Damned offensive, sir, if you ask

me." Here he would square his fine old
shoulders, and light a fire in his dark blue
eyes, with the ridiculous effect that he looked
younger than his youngest son. But you
couldn't stop them. The Baroness, also,
was "the inexpressible She" or "the ship-
launcher" in allusion to her name. I remember that at the moment of her coming into
the hall for dinner, the first night of the visit,
Patrick whispered to me, "Was *this* the
face...?" and added afterwards to a younger
friend, "By Gad, it might be." He was much
impressed, as they all were, by her charm
of quiet. All this speculative pleasantry was
flying about *ad libitum*, before they came.
Hector, that ostrich, buried his head, and
gave the rest of himself away. He used to
speak of Helena with elaborate unconcern,
as if he hadn't thought of her much up to
now. "Good-looking? Yes, I fancy you
would call her good-looking—in a placid, sort
of nun-like way." He infuriated Pierpoint
by that. "Look here, Hector," that flushed
and really noble-looking youth cried out at
him, "are you going to sit there and tell
me she's demure?" Hector said that he

was going to sit there and tell him nothing.
Patrick suggested that perhaps she was
"arch." Wynyard, who was eating muffins,
said that we should try the Knockacarrig
beat to-morrow. The wind was right. He
couldn't see what use there was in discussing
the appearance of a woman who wasn't there
and whom nobody but Hector had seen.
Patrick jumped up to confute him. If, he
said, she *was* there, you naturally couldn't
discuss her, and if everybody had seen her
it wouldn't be worth while. What did Wynyard say to that? Wynyard said nothing
to it, but finished the muffins, and then asked
if anybody would play squash with him before
dinner. That was how they went on all the
time, sparring and wrangling. But they were
very close-knit for all that. It meant nothing.
If you touched one of them you touched the
whole pack, and Sir Roderick first of all.
There was something fine about that old
giant when he was in a rage. You forgot
how stupid he was.

Hector set great store by this visit of his
lady and her grim possessor. He made me

his confessor shortly after I came, telling me
that when he left me in Milan in the spring
he had indeed gone home—but by way of
Venice and Vienna! There he had been in
her company for two clear days. She had
not been offended—far from it. She had never
been kinder to him than she had then proved
herself. Heavenly creature! he said, she had
seemed to know that he would come: she
had seemed touched by it. That a woman
should be grateful to you for what is the act
of sheer self-gratification! Can anything be
more beautifully condescending than that?
It is innate courtesy of the most exquisite
refinement. And not a cloud in the sky—
not a cloud! She gave up all her engage-
ments on his account. They spent their days
in the galleries—the evenings in her fine
house. There were people there, of course—
a soft-footed priest with a white head, he
told me, a Monsignore who seemed to be a
relative of hers; a Miss Waggetts who was
governess to Hermione; a mysterious old
black-browed lady with a name like Korsaczy,
who always looked as if a thunder-storm was
going on in the top of her head. That was

because she blinked. You thought of lightning. Helena didn't explain any of these
people to him, nor (he supposed) himself to
them. She had a way of murmuring names
in the air, and leaving them to be sorted by
their owners. He laughed the laugh of a
lover: "I adore her dependence on Providence," he said, "but she is undeniably vague
sometimes. The Korsaczy didn't catch my
name at all, and had it out of me afterwards.
She didn't like it when she had it. She said
it sounded like a curse. Malison—do you
see? Clever of her. The *tu quoque* was
obvious, but I let it go. She didn't like me,
but that didn't matter....It was beautiful
to see her—I mean Helena—with Hermione.
A tall, creamy-skinned, grave child with her
mother's deep grey eyes and cloudy hair.
Nothing was said of the satyr—bah! we
won't talk of him. Hermione used to lean
against her mother's knee while I was there
talking; and every now and then they used
to look at each other and smile. It was like
the sun breaking out; one used to wait for
it. . . . The second of my days she touched
me to the point of tears. It was after luncheon.

6

I was following them out of the room, and
in the corridor Hermione waited for me, and
held out her hand. We went on handfasted.
A child's confidence is worth having. That
makes a man think himself somebody." I
agreed with him.

There was more to come. I knew that and
waited for it. Presently he said, "Her patience
is exquisite. It's so beautiful that sometimes
I think what she goes through may be worth
while—to secure it to her, don't you see?
You know how I look upon Beauty, as being
so much the assurance of a virtue that it
becomes a virtue in itself. It follows that
any indignity offered to Beauty—especially
Spiritual Beauty, as Helena's is—is a thing
unendurable; it's like winking at obscenity;
it's like allowing immorality in your own
house. I had a long talk with her about that
—I couldn't say much, naturally—but she
knew what I meant. I said that a man knows
that he's a good poet, or linguist, or chemist,
and takes his stand in the world on that
ground. It seemed to me that a woman
must know not only the fact of her beauty,
but also the rights due to it. Without vanity

she seeks to enhance it, taking thought for
her clothes, her hair, and things like that.
Is she not entitled to say to the world: 'This
beauty of mine, which you admit by your
words, you shall admit also by your acts?
No man in the world has a right over it
but by free grant from me.' I didn't put
it so crudely as that—I didn't dot the
i's or cross all the *t's*—but I took pains
about it.

"She was very gentle with me. I think
that she was moved. She said that I had
high standards, which were not common.
In her country, she said, men talked like that
before they married, but that, being married,
they only talked so to other men's wives.
I told her that England stood in no better
case; but did all this matter? Could brutish
behaviour alter eternal laws? She sighed
as she said that custom had the force of law.
And then, as if to end the discussion, she
bent over her netting and said, 'You mustn't
be unhappy. I shall be disappointed if I
think that you go home unhappy. I promise
you that I shall remember our talks, and be
the more contented for them. I haven't many

friends—but I count upon your friendship.
It is a great thing for me.'

"Upon my soul, I dared not say any more.
She asked me not to write to her often—not
more than twice, she said. It was understood
that they were to come here. I think I
wrote three times. She answered one letter
of mine—but that's all."

"Do you think—?" I began to ask him
a question which I might have had some
difficulty in completing. But he answered
it as it was.

"No, I don't. I don't think she has any
love of that kind for anybody. I think she
is too out of the world for love, as the world
understands it. I doubt if the feelings of
ordinary women mean anything to her. But
I do think that she is pleased with me. She
listens to me, and thinks about what I say.
Yes, I do think so."

"What do you suppose *he* thinks about it,
Hector?" I asked him.

"I don't know," he said, "and don't care,
at present. He may be troublesome later on."

I pressed him. "What do you mean—
later on?"

"I mean," he said, "when he knows what I am up to—and that I don't mean to leave him alone."

I deprecated. "Really, I don't know how you can keep his company," I said. "Mind you, he's very intelligent."

"Oh, damnably," said Hector. "But so is she."

"Well, my dear chap?"

Hector got up and plunged his hands into his pockets. "Well, it's got to this. She is used to him. He's horrible, but she's used to him and his horrors. And now—well—now she has begun to find out that she ought not to be."

I looked at him. "You mean to say that you've laid a drawn sword——?"

He met me. "I mean to say that I have proved to her own conviction that she is a beautiful woman," he said—and then, "We must go and dress."

I don't seek to excuse my friend; indeed, I suppose that if he was in love with Helena von Broderode he is to be excused for his intromission in her private affairs. It didn't, at the time, seem to me to amount to much. Not to more than this, perhaps, that it amounted to just as much or just as little as she chose to make it stand for. And after all is said and done, hedges only exist in love to be broken through. The state of his feelings magnified the offences of the unfortunate Baron—offences, mind you, that were mere guess work on Hector's part; they magnified also the distress of the Baroness—guess-work again. My distinct opinion is that the Baroness wasn't particularly uncomfortable with her Baron's attentions until she found Hector scandalized about it. She had been married twelve years. The Baron's malady didn't attack him until half that time had expired. I doubt her extreme sensibility. I think she was of a placid nature, if you ask me. I felt very strongly at the time that if distress existed in the Baroness it was almost entirely because Hector had put it there. I am bound to say that that was wanton of him, too bad; and I don't think that any flummery about the sovereign rights of Beauty will excuse a man making a beauty uncomfortable. I beg Hector's pardon. Hector was a poet, it may be—for you can be a poet without making any poems. I imagine that Beauty was to him a very tangible thing—a kind of gloss upon things and persons (mostly persons, I am bound to say, and mostly, too, female persons) which might be, in his eyes, visibly tarnished. But the plain truth is, Hector's idealism of beauty was pure sex—nothing else at all. If it had not been so, there was his brother Pierpoint, for example—the most beautiful creature in these islands—a miracle of grace and strength, the perfection of line and colour, and rare blood and high spirit: a creature like a god. Yet Hector never saw beauty like a gloss upon him. No, no. He was in love with Helena— as well he might be; he was in love with her after his own—as I think—rather anæmic fashion. He perched her up on a five-foot pedestal—so that her head was at least ten feet in the air. And then he called out to the world in general, "I have found a woman who is ten feet high. She must be an immortal. Come, we will turn her into a church. No man must smoke a cigar, or spit, or scratch his head, or go to sleep near her. One does

not do these things in churches, and I tell
you that you are in church where she is."
That's how sex takes you. Sheer sex: nothing
else at all.

I couldn't say this to him, .and it would
have been little use if I had. As things turned
out, I am glad that I did not, for the very
peculiar twist in Hector's nature made him
fairly comfortable in the most uncomfortable
position—without any exception—in which
amorous man ever found himself. But one
thing at a time. We haven't reached that
yet.

In days to come I remembered that talk
with Hector. It was the night before the
von Broderodes were due.

And I remember another thing not at the
time memorable. I remember coming out
of my room and passing Pierpoint's on my
way to the staircase. Just before I reached
his door it opened, but nobody came out.
I heard his voice saying with emphasis, "No,
not to-night. It's out of the question. You
know that as well as I do." Then I suppose
my steps were heard: the door was closed
again, and held-to until I had turned the

corner by the stair. On the way down-stairs Pierpoint, coming three at a time, bumped into me and saved himself by clinging round my neck. "Frightfully sorry," he panted. "You see, I thought I was late. And you know what the governor is. Balked of his prey!"

"Come on," I said, "we'll brazen it out between us. I heard you as I passed your door. You were rather positive, I thought. I was on the point of looking in."

He gave me a sharp look. For a second or two it was intense. Then he laughed. "Quite as well you didn't, old chap." That was what he said.

VI

THE STATE VISIT

SIR RODERICK was a dear old man, whose besetting sin was vanity. He had been a splendid specimen of mankind in his day—and he still was the perfection of hale, frosty, alert old age—and I suspect that his excessive partiality for Pierpoint sprang from that. He renewed his youth in that hero; he saw himself in his acts, and all the admiration which the youth won for himself—which was inordinate—he applied like ointment to his own old person. But that is parenthesis. One of the by-products of his vanity was that in order to magnify himself he had to magnify everything to do with himself. His stags had to be bigger than any other man's stags; his gillies tougher than any other man's gillies; his housemaids better looking than any other man's housemaids. One of them certainly was, by the way: Ethel Cook was her name. She was supposed to be the best-looking housemaid in the world. I remember that

90

he was bragging about the maids at Inveroran
one day—how good they were, how long
they stayed, what fine girls and all that. It
was after breakfast. He and I were in the
hall. "You shall see for yourself," he said.
He rang the bell and told the man to fetch
Ethel. I couldn't tell him—hadn't the heart—
that I knew all about her, that she was famous
in her way. He must have known that I had
danced with her at the servants' ball every
year since she had been there—but nothing
would do. Down she must come. By and
by, sure enough, down she came. Undoubtedly she was magnificent—about five foot
eight, with a fine, small head on her shoulders,
and a grave, self-possessed pair of grey eyes.
He gave her an order about something or
other, and kept her for a while talking. She
was perfectly respectful, but not at all uneasy.
Then he sent her off. "That young woman
has been here for seven years," he told me.
I knew she had. "She came at sixteen."
I knew that too. "She's now twenty-three.
I respect her, sir. She's made herself respected.
And look at her. She's one of the family.
She declines to marry, though half the men

in the place would go through the fire for
her. But no! And she comes from the
South—a Gloucestershire girl. Now, they
are all of that pattern. Let me tell you
this . . ." and then the dear old gas-bag
puffed out his chest, and stroked his beard,
and went off again.

That is another parenthesis, which I must
be excused. What I am coming to is that,
owing to this little weakness of his—of magni-
fying himself in his circumstance—there was
some danger, perfectly visible to the family,
of his turning the von Broderode visit into
an act of international courtesy. He might
very easily have had the town be-flagged.
Triumphal arches were talked of, and the
German dictionary got out. Patrick staved
that off by insisting on Polish—for the Baroness. He said that it wasn't like his father to
ignore the rights of a crushed and beaten
race. "Do you think," he said, "that she
don't get enough German rubbed into her
in Galicia? And you expect her to come here
and find German inscriptions?" That was
the way to get at him—to be as literal as
himself. Sir Roderick was touched. "You

are right, my lad," he said. "It would be a
great want of tact. No, no. That would never
do." So we got off the arches. But the whole
course of a week bristled with pitfalls. Should
there be an address at the station? Should
he himself be on the platform? A red baize,
now? The pipes?

One thing he had so set his heart on that
it stabbed us to ours to deny it him. He
saw a group of us all on the steps to await
the carriage—himself in the midst of his tall
sons—guests in wicker chairs—Lord Mark in
his yeomanry uniform—then men holding
dogs in leashes—the servants in white caps,
or with livery buttons looking like pills on
the photograph—! It was to be like the
pictures of the German Emperor at a wedding.
Really, he was so unhappy when the boys
flatly refused, one after the other, that I was
fool enough to say I'd do it, and Lady Mark
backed me up and went so far as to say she
would like it. But the boys were of sterner
stuff. Patrick said he'd do it on one condition, which was that he should wear his
bathing suit and carry a parasol. Pierpoint
and Wynyard, the twins, should sit at each

corner in huge turn-down collars—perhaps
with banjoes. The poor old dear saw that
it was no go, and gave it up. "It would have
been a graceful act, sir," he said to me.
"That was how we received the late King—
and the King was pleased. He as good as
said so. But, however—" He was dreadfully hurt, very stately and remote to Pat,
pressed the port on me—told me its year
and all that—offered me a cigar! In fact, he
sulked in a very dignified way all dinner-time.

After a series of pounding defeats like this
we became magnanimous and let him win a
couple of outpost skirmishes. He was allowed
the great carriage instead of the motor.
Hector went down in it to please him. And
the Castle pipers were at the station with
their bags of tricks under their arms. We
even let him have that. Being a Southron
myself, like Miss Ethel Cook, I saw no religious significance in these chaps, and got all
the more pleasure out of them. I love them
above all on these sort of days of pomp.
They always bring me tears. I can see them
now in that breezy, dusty station yard, stalk-

ing up and down like high-stepping cocks, or standing together, discoursing of great affairs with each other, in an open-mouthed circle of bare-footed boys. And when the train was signalled, the toss of the head as each met the other's eye! And when it was in sight, the long wheeze of preparation! And then the outburst—the crash, the triumphant scream—and the march away up the street! I love it, I tell you—and it nearly always makes me cry. I think that fair Helena was moved too. As for the Baron, I'll swear that he didn't miss anything. He never did.

Our part up at the house—since the whole thing had got on our nerves—was to be as unconcerned as possible. We would *not* be on the steps. Sir Roderick should have them to himself. Those of us who were at home— all the men except myself and Hector were on the moors, and a good many of the women obstinately sat in the hall with the tea-things. Lady Mark—as bad as any of us by now—insisted on my playing draughts with her. She said it would look "informal"; she thought it would "put them at their ease."

Amusing way of putting the cool cucumber
at his ease!   He might be trusted to do that
for himself.

When Sir Roderick brought her in, Lady
Mark's informality ceased. She was much
too interested in Hector's "passion," as she
called Helena. She saw instantly that she
was all right—and she certainly was. I'm no
good at lady's dresses—broad effects for me.
I content myself by recording that it was
black and white, that it seemed to drape her
and be unwilling to leave her, if you understand me. It looked to me very expensive.
Then she had an early Victorian hat, a long,
drooping, flagged affair, with a black feather.
It was very big and very black. It set her
pale face off—it made that look like a moon
steering through a dark rain-cloud. And there
was Hector, adoring her from a respectful
distance in the background! She knew it:
and how immensely touched and gratified she
was with it all! So much for that. She
smiled a very friendly greeting to me and
allowed me to kiss her hand—anyhow, that
is what I took upon me to do. She was quite
self-possessed and, if I may say so, ready for

anything. She felt herself, very pardonably, to be making an effective entrance. Every woman knows that kind of thing.

Hector waited upon the Baron, as I supposed; and pretty soon I heard the two sticks and guessed at the dragging glide. At the open door he stood to rest, propped upon them, confronting the citadel, as it were, with the gallant and weathered eye of an old campaigner. Here he was then—up against it. He must have known it. He took us all in at a glance; he sized the whole thing up. He was hard put to it for his breath, I guess; but he masked his fatigue with that dauntless smile of his which always endeared him to me, ghoul or no ghoul. A cool cucumber indeed was the Baron von Broderode.

And how he played up at the tea-table! How he massed his forces for the attack on his traitor tell-tale hands, how he was beaten, how he returned to the assault again and again! How he talked, joked, relished everything through what must have been devastating efforts! After all, a man with a zest like that *was* a man. Lady Mark told me afterwards that she thought him a *dangerous*

man, because, forsooth, "he took so much
for granted." I discovered after a bit what
she meant. He had taken her nationality
for granted. He told her in a few minutes
that he knew America, and even surmised
that she came from New England—which, in
fact, she did. I suppose it was a shot; but
it was just like him (a) to have made it, (b)
to have been right. Mrs. Vane, too, who was
the wife of the money-hunting Colonel—he
was ready for her. He told her he had met a
Captain Vane in India—and gave the year.
It was the Colonel! You couldn't get away
from the Baron anywhere, even on the wings
of the morning.

After tea, although it was getting dusk,
Sir Roderick had them out into the gardens.
The Baron excused himself and retired to his
rooms, where I suppose his man and his Teresa
had got things snug for him. He had brought
his Teresa. Helena went off between father
and son; and in due course we all took our
ways. The shooters came in late, and her
first public appearance was before dinner.

They were all assembled when she came
down-stairs. Even the Baron had got himself

down before her. She not only looked very beautiful, but extremely young for her thirty. It was then that Patrick said that hers might be the face that had the ships

Crowded in Aulis like white birds.

She was in black—with the family diamonds, or some of them, in her hair.

Sir Roderick, with his infallible eye for stage-sentiment, had his young men about him, and presented them formally. Bearded, red Wynyard—"our mighty hunter, Baroness," then Pierpoint, "like some hot amorist" —"and this is my scapegrace, Pierpoint," who said, "You do me honour, sir," and stooped burning bright over her. I saw her look up with her friendly smile—and then I saw her eyes flicker and fall. Then came Patrick, who introduced himself —"I'm Patrick—how do you do?" He spared the rest of them. Lady Mark presented her lord, who bowed, and received a bow. Then the pipes burst out—the Baron said "Ha!" very loud, and we proceeded to dinner.

Dinner was rather heavy, I thought. There was too much of the banquet about it. Sir

Roderick might have been the Lord Mayor entertaining royalty. There was nothing of the modern light hand about the old chief. On her other side there was Lord Mark, who did his best. You could describe Lord Mark best in wine-merchant language, as a perfect table wine, "very light and dry." Hector was solemn, rather like a sweet port; Wynyard ate his food, and Pierpoint was bored. I had a girl to look after who had hitherto been at one of the round tables where the young things kept up their brisk cannonades of small jokes and bread pills. I too did my best; but she looked over her shoulder more than once, and more than once wondered "what they were doing." I advised her finally to go there on all-fours and find out. She liked the idea, but funked it.

By far the best company was the Baron. He never gave in; he ate of everything; drank champagne; made jokes and laughed at them; told anecdotes across the table; you never saw a man so much at ease in the midst of struggles which would have worn down Antæus. I didn't know whether to envy the more his spirit or his zest. Pierpoint

interested him because of his perfections—
I could see that. He talked across Lady
Mark, and when the young man's attention
wandered, he brought it back again by talking
at him. He was evidently studying Pierpoint,
and I wondered if he had seen that conquering
glance before which his fair wife had abased
her eyes. Was it possible that the Baron was
a jealous husband? I certainly had reason
to ask as time went on, because it became
evident to everybody, almost from the start,
that Pierpoint was out for scalps.

When we joined the ladies, things went
much better. The bridge players roped in
the Baron, as I knew they would. The heroic
man assented, and I fancy that Colonel Vane
dropped money. He had told me before
dinner that he had won ten shillings off
Patrick, on the moors, for two right-and-lefts
running. "And, by Gad, I wanted it!"— he
had not failed to add. But I believe that he
met his match in the Baron.

As for the others, there was to be a rag,
Patrick said—and there was a rag. We played
all sorts of foolish games. I only remember

forfeits because I have a vision of Pierpoint
kneeling on one knee before Helena and telling
her that she must "do something" to him.

She looked adorable—confused and happy
at once. Her eyes very bright and kind.
"What must I do to you?" she asked him.

He didn't shirk it. "You may do any
mortal thing you like to me," he said.

She hesitated, seemed to hover over him,
then put her hand lightly on his shoulder for a
minute and let it stay there.

"The accolade," she told him.

"I am your knight, then," he said, "Knight
of St. Helena." Then he got up. It was
really very pretty.

VII

SETTLING IN

I HAD work to do which kept me at the desk all my mornings, so I am not clear as to the immediate course of events. There was great play, from the very beginning, but I can't be sure how it went. So far as I could judge from a few casual glimpses, or a gibe or two let fly by the youths, Pierpoint made the running. He was, of course, the beauty, and he founded himself upon that. Even Pat acknowledged a kind of *droit de seigneur* in his glowing brother. But the fact is that they took her to the family heart from the beginning, and to find out why they did would be a curious inquiry. My own belief is that it was because she was so evidently pleased to be there. Nothing pleases people so much as to discover that they are pleasing. That makes you enthusiastic. You say, What a delightful girl! She likes me! Every Malleson of them, I think, felt like that about Helena—from the chief, who adored women,

especially young ones, and would have given
up his kingdom for a daughter, down to
Patrick the insipient, who, for the matter
of that, liked everybody. I used to see her
dance away in the mornings with a whole
bevy of them about her, to see dogs, or to
bathe, or sail, as the case might be; and it
was delightful to note her intense appreciation
of the flickering, random, high-spirited pack.
If the chief went with them she used to effect
sedateness and stay behind to talk, or rather
to hear him talk. He showed her views, trees
planted by crowned heads, funeral mounds
of old horses, dogs' tombstones, and all the
rest of it. She bent him filial attention—
and he revelled in it. Once she went off for
a walk with Hector; but only once, so far
as I know. I used to imagine that she and
Hector had an understanding by which they
could take each other's feelings for granted
—but I'm not so sure about it now. Wynyard
was the dark horse of the lot. He took her
very bluntly after his manner. The more
he had liked her the less he would have shown
it. I knew that and used to watch for it.
I noticed a curt address of her once or twice.

She was considering whether she should go
out with the shooters. He said he didn't
think it was the place for women. I saw her
bite her lip.

As for the Baron, they fitted him up with
a pony and took him out every day. I understood from Wynyard, who was an expert,
that he did very well. "Gets his gun up like
lightning and fires at the instant. He's a
sportsman." This was high praise from Wynyard, and a long speech from the silent man
of the house. But the Baron was a great
success, and I gathered from his expansion
at dinner that he knew it, and that all went
well with him. He, too, pleased, and was
pleased.

She, oddly enough, did not do so well with
the women. They were a little bit cool to
her, it seemed. Lady Mark said that she
was secretive. I don't quite know what she
meant, unless it was that Helena didn't
choose to talk about her admirers as if they
were pet dogs. The girls, too, were a little
bit jealous: perhaps they thought her too
young for her age—and perhaps, poor dear,
she was. She had every excuse if, as I expect,

she had never been young before. Hector
took her out riding one or two days, but not
alone; one day she was on the moors—at
Wynyard's invitation. She marched about
with guns, lunched at a sheeling, and was
rather bored. That may have been because
shooting under Wynyard's marshalling was
apt to be so mighty serious. She confessed
to Hector afterwards that she didn't like to
see things killed, although she thought we
did it as kindly as it could be done. She was
greatly struck by British kindness, and disposed to trust it a very long way. She told
me that in a half-hour of expansion. "I
have never been in England before—" she
began, and I thought I had better tell her
that she wasn't in England now. "No, no,"
she said, "I know—I have made that blunder
already. Patrick stopped me. I hope Sir
Roderick didn't hear me. But at home we
have the habit of talking of you all as the
English."

"We'll let it pass this time," I said, and
then invited her to proceed.

She said, "I am lost in admiration at two
things. First, that you are so good-looking,

and next that you are so gentle. I think it
is because you are proud. It seems beneath
your dignity to be savage, or to speak disdain-
fully to servants."

I said that I thought we were rather slack
than proud. "It's not worth while being
angry with a servant. The great thing is to
let them alone. If that don't answer, they
must go. That's how we look at it, I think."

She wasn't listening, but seemed lost in
reverie. Then she said, "They are awfully
kind to me—and all for nothing, but gentle-
ness!"

I said, "It would be very hard to be anything but gentle in your case."

She was pleased. "Ah," she said, "you
have no idea how grateful I am for kindness.
It touches me deeply—always."

"Surely," I said, "you must be prepared
for that."

She misunderstood me. "You mean—by
Mr. Malleson—Mr. Hector? Yes, indeed. I
think he has very noble ideals. He seems to
me a beautiful nature—but——"

I waited.

"But—" she didn't know how to put it—

then gave it up. "Tell me about the others. What do they do? Do they always lead this happy life? Have they no professions? One is in the marine, I think? That is Mr. Nigel, who is not here?" I nodded. "Then one is in Orders—in our Church?"

"Yes," I said. "Spenser Malleson's a priest. And a missionary at that. He's out in China, waiting for the toasting-fork."

"And Mr. Wynyard—what does Mr. Wynyard do when he is not killing?"

I laughed. "He prepares to kill. He does nothing else. But he's a great naturalist. He kills in kindness. He's awfully fond of birds, really. You may not agree, but that's why he's such a good shot."

She said, "I would agree if I understood." After a bit she said, with a quite perceptible taking of breath, "And Pierpoint—Mr. Pierpoint?"

"Pierpoint," I told her, "is a soldier. He's cavalry—a Lancer. But he's on leave now. He's a fine-looking boy, don't you think?"

She looked down. "He is very handsome. I don't think I have ever seen a man so handsome. But you call him a boy?"

"I call him a boy," I said, "because I am forty-two."

She looked up. "And he is—?"

"I don't know to a year how old Pierpoint is," I said, though it wasn't true. "But he is not forty-two, I assure you.'

She laughed. "No, indeed. But one sees he is not a boy."

"No, no," I said. "It was only a figure of speech. He is full-grown."

There we came to a stop about Pierpoint— or it seemed so. She made a wide cast, and began again on Hector.

"Mr. Hector," she said, "is very unlike his brothers."

"Yes," I admitted. "He is unlike all that you see here. Physically, he's like Patrick. Don't you see it? They favor their mother's family. She was Lord Mark's sister. Morally, he's like Spenser, the priest. An enthusiast, an idealist of a rather pronounced type. Everything is either coal-black or snow-white to Hector. He don't know the word compromise. But he's very pussy about it. He keeps quiet till he's wanted—or thinks that he's wanted."

Her eyes shone. "Yes, that is so true. I wished to ask you about that. As you say, he is very quiet, very gentle. But these others—they are strong, they are swift and proud. They are like their father—what a fine man he is! He knows that he is a king. He walks the world as if it was his. But when Hector is head of the house—or as he is now, the heir of it—how does he exert authority? Or has he no authority over them? Do they listen to his advice? Do they obey him? He is so quiet!"

I laughed—not derisively at all—appreciatively rather. "Yes, he is quiet," I said. "You might call him mild. But they know better. I feel sure—I know—that when he takes Sir Roderick's place he will have the power which Sir Roderick has. If he were to say to Wynyard, 'Look here, it is absolutely necessary for my health that you should drown yourself to-morrow morning in the bay,' Wynyard would do it."

She said, "You are laughing at me."

I assured her that I was not. "It's an extreme case, of course, but the principle is sound. Convince one of these fellows that

it is up to him to do something for Hector's
sake—he'll do it. He must."

She took that very seriously. She liked
it.

I went on. "Mind you, there's the other
side of the proposition, which is equally binding. I know that Hector would go the same
lengths for one of them. He would stick at
nothing. He would see it as his duty. He
would stick at nothing on earth. And, of
course, they know that. Both terms of the
proposition are in the blood. They've been
bred to it."

She had me then. "Do you think that the
priest would be like that—like the others?"
That was clever of her.

I said, "Spenser is a priest. He's not a
Jesuit, but they reared him. That's an iron
system. I won't answer for Spenser. But
I'll tell you this: Hector might think it his
duty to be burned at the stake for Spenser—
and burned he would be."

She thanked me for talking to her, which
I assured her she needn't have done. It was
exciting to watch her as she listened and
thrilled. She was like some beautiful insect

—with new wings quivering in the light. I wondered what would happen to her with Hector on one side of her, Pierpoint on the other—and the grim old Baron drinking cigar-smoke against the wall.

After a bit the positions began to shift and develop themselves. Pierpoint openly paid court to her, and Hector wasn't happy. That was clear enough to anybody. Old Miss Bacchus, who came up a day or two after the von Broderodes, took it all in the first night she was there. She went everywhere, as they say, and knew everybody. She was a hideous lady, with a red front of somebody else's hair—"another man's hair," as Patrick put it—but there was no nonsense about her. When we went into the drawing-room, and Pierpoint, as his custom now was, went straight to Helena and sat by her, as if she belonged to him, Hector stood with his back to the fire and looked unutterable things. Miss Bacchus came and plumped down by me.

"I say," she began, "I don't know what all this is about—do you?"

I said, "All what?" But it wouldn't do.

"My dear man," she said, "why put it off? I'm like the dentist. You'll feel better afterwards."

I said, "I've a horror of your gouges. You call it moral pressure, I know. You should let a poor beggar alone. I never did you any harm."

"Look at her," said Miss Bacchus, and I did. "You know," she went on, "that woman has never been made a fuss about before; and she likes it—she likes it awfully. She'll lose her head—that's what she'll do. And Pierpoint's no good, you know. He's a rogue."

"Not a roguey-poguey, I trust," I said.

"No," she said, "that's the female of rogue. Now Hector wouldn't do her any harm."

"Wouldn't he?" I didn't want to discuss my friend's affairs with this too candid dame.

At this moment, without any warning, she fetched me a crack on the knee with her fan. "You talk to Hector," she said. "He's your friend. You ought to."

"I'll tell him what you say," I told her. She snorted.

8

"For twopence I'd talk to him myself.
But he wouldn't listen to me. He'd say it
wasn't honourable."

"Well," I said, "there's something in that,
you know."

Miss Bacchus scorned me. "You talk like
Mr. Brooke. Honour be blowed. Look at
Pierpoint. What does he think about? He's
like a little dog or a little boy—he thinks of
what he wants, and nothing else."

"That sort get on," I said.

"That sort get run over at a crossing pretty
often," said Miss Bacchus.

"Baron von Broderode likes both of them,"
I told her. "But he likes Pierpoint best."

Miss Bacchus gave me a cool stare. "Is
that your little idea?" she said. "Well, let
me tell you that you are dead wrong. The
Baron dislikes Pierpoint extremely."

"My dear friend, how *do* you know that?"
I asked her.

"Because," she said, "he is so friendly
with him. Don't you see that the Baron
never shirks a thing? Don't you see that
he comes to terms with it—whether it's a
man after his wife, or a locomotor ataxy after

him—he'll never compromise. Come on, he
says, let's have a look at you. God bless
me, where are your eyes?"

"They are upon you," I said, "with admiration and envy. You have been in his company about two hours and a half. You have
never exchanged a word with him. But you
have got him in spirits.''

"No, I haven't," she said with head-
shaking; "no, my dear man, I haven't.
He's got himself in 'em. Nobody in this
house is going to get the Baron. Don't you
make any mistake. Now, I'll tell you something. He's in the next room playing bridge,
isn't he? Very well. Now I'll undertake
to say that he could give you a chart showing
where *she* is, where Pierpoint is, and where
Hector is. Although he's seen nothing of
'em! . . . . And another thing. I'll bet you
half-a-crown that before the Broderodes go
the Baron will ask Pierpoint to come and
shoot with him in Galicia. Do you take
that?"

I said that I would rather not. The odd
part of the tale is that the Baron did ask
him.

She was a good old soul, though. I watched
her with amazement go directly from me to
the other end of the room and plump herself
down beside Helena. I thought that the
beauty was annoyed—and she might very
well have been so; but she had very pretty
manners. Miss Bacchus "butted in," as Lady
Mark would say, with the utmost gallantry,
and (as I could see) brought Pierpoint smartly
to heel in a few rounds. After a little more
she beckoned Hector over with a toss of her
head, and I saw the poor chap swallow his
mortification and be all the better for it.
Pierpoint got sick of it and took himself off.
We saw no more of him. And then Miss
Bacchus, her fairy godmothership accomplished, limped away on her own account.
I was delighted to receive a friendly wink
as she passed me. "Cooked *his* goose for
him," she said—in what she thought, no
doubt, was a whisper.

Helena was being quite kind to Hector.
Evidently she thought that she had mis-
behaved.

Now I come to the ball—but must have
a new chapter for it.

VIII

EUPHEMIA

IT was a yearly business, the Inveroran Ball. It always followed the Highland Gathering; and after it there was a servants' ball. All these were great spectacles for the Baron, who prepared himself for them with German thoroughness, but also with a southern brightness which belongs only to his branch of the Teuton family. He read a book upon the clans, and got to know the tartans. He said to me, "They are like the Greeks, these Gaels —like Greeks in the rain. You have the clan Nestor, the clan Tydeus, the clan Peleus, the clan Atreus. But you have no Homer to sing of them. You have Ossian—who weeps and has a hump." He never got the argot quite right. "Yes, that is right," he chuckled. "Ossian has a hump, and the reader wants an umbrella." He was very pleased with that, but I told him that the Highland Gathering would produce no umbrellas. He wanted to know about the Gathering. I said that it was very like the games in Scheria when Odysseus scored off the Phæacians. "So!" said the Baron. "But Odysseus, where is he?" We exchanged looks, and he shrugged his great shoulders. "Once," he said, "I could have been he. Now I am what you see." It was the only time, during my acquaintance with him, that he ever admitted incapacity. He did it without any trace of bitterness: I don't think he felt any grudge against Providence. He would have been the first to admit that he had had his whack.

He was always very friendly with me, and seemed to find me provocative of jocularity; I don't know why, unless it was a reminiscence of Chevenix, who had been in my company when we first met. Chevenix had a way of impressing himself on the tourist. He had a very pronounced voice and his anecdotes were often intimate. "As your gold-tipt friend would say," was the Baron's signal for a laborious pleasantry. So it was that when it was arranged he should ride his pony down to the meeting, he asked me to ride with him.

We went down therefore together. They held the sports in a great field between Oran-

mouth and the town. It was called the Port
Field and ran up to the edge of the moors
in a fine amphitheatre of foothills. Ben Mor,
the great mountain of these parts, filled the
distance with rock and cloud.

"You English," said he, "are a strange race. I
suppose you have not possessed the Highlands
for more than two hundred, two hundred-
fifty years, but already you have taught
the Highlander to play at life. What is Sir
Roderick but a white-bearded schoolboy?
Is it not so?"

I said that Sir Roderick had been educated
in England, but at bottom was quite un-
English.

"And his sons—!" The Baron threw up
his whip hand. "These fine young men—do
they not play?"

I admitted that they did; but I added that
they worked at it.

"Yes, that is true. As your friend would
say, they work at their play, and they play at
their work. You can't tell one from the
other."

"No," I agreed, "you can't. And that's
why they work so well. There's *gusto* there."

That set him nodding his head and frowning. He knew all about *gusto*.

When we were pacing down the main street his eyes were all about. He noticed the little poky shops; he was tickled by the holystone patterns on the thresholds. He was pleased with the way private houses were interspersed with places of business. "There," he said, as we passed Rosemount, "is a pretty doll's house."

Rosemount is just that. A white house with a green slate roof; a neat little forecourt of green turf divided by a brick-on-edge path. An auraucaria on one side, an Irish yew on the other; a little white gate; red blinds, half-drawn, in all the windows. Charming with the gleam of sunlight shining on wet slates and splashing half the face. I told him that they called it Naboth's Vineyard at·the Castle.

"So!" he said, and frowned over the name.

I explained that it was the only house in the whole town—the only house in the whole district—which did not belong to the Mallesons. It involved a long story—about a mistress of Sir Alastair Malleson, who had it given her and used it to affront the lady he

subsequently married. Euphemia Grant her
name was, and it had belonged to her family
ever since. The story was picturesque because of its excrescence. A blight upon our
host's family was believed to depend upon it.

The Baron, greatly interested, pulled up his
pony. "Tell me that story, if you please,"
he said, and fixed me with his eye.

The story very shortly was that Sir Alastair,
who afterwards went out in the '45 and was
shot at Derby from behind a hedge, had in his
roaming days carried off Euphemia Grant and
kept her at the Castle. There she reigned
until he took a wife. Euphemia's people,
who had been quite in a small way, instead of
disowning her, as you might have expected,
took her back again, and set her up in Rosemount as a thorn in the side of Sir Alastair.
She was known to the country as Madam
Grant, and grew to be much respected for her
implacability. She never married, but lived
at Rosemount alone when, in the course of
nature and the law, the place was left to her.
On her death-bed she cursed the Mallesons,
declaring that there would never be a daughter to the house again while Rosemount

stood. The odd thing was that there never had been. Sir Alastair's wife had two sons, but no daughter. His successor, Sir Archibald, had no children at all. Sir Ronald had sons and a daughter who died a child; and so it had gone on until here was Sir Roderick a widower with a regiment of sons and no daughter. One might laugh, in England, at such things; but they didn't laugh in Scotland. Sir Roderick believed in it as he did in the Old Testament. He had so far demeaned himself as to write with his own hand to the owner of Rosemount. He would give anything you please for the place. But the Grants persisted, and could not be moved. An old Peter Grant held it now; but he was a Glasgow merchant and never occupied it. Nothing would induce him to sell it.

The Baron seemed to think this absurd. In his country, he said, they would make short work of Peter Grant. I asked him, How? lightly enough, and a very odd thing occurred. I saw him suddenly transported with rage. His eyes flashed fire; he was purplish red in the face. He shook his fist at the sky. "How?" he trumpeted. "How? Why, we squeeze him!" *Shkveeze him!*—I can't find signs to express it. But the concentration of shuddering rage which he put into it would pass your belief. I was astounded, and he saw I was, for he instantly laughed it off. "The damned fellow!" he said lightly, and began to talk of something else. I thought about this outburst for a long time. I am quite sure that he wanted to squeeze somebody, and equally clear that it wasn't Peter Grant.

He was all smiles and nods and becks at the Gathering, however. He was introduced to the local Marchioness, and stayed it out to the last. I think he would have seen the fireworks with a little encouragement. Wynyard, as usual, tossed the pine-stem. I saw the Baron look wistful. He rode across the field to shake hands with him for that; and Wynyard thanked him.

The day ended with a sort of enthronization of Helena. She gave away the prizes, and did it charmingly. Without a hint to the purpose, by the intuition which all nice women have, she made the little speeches to the agonists which mean so much to them. Pierpoint got one, Wynyard, of course, two, and several fine blue-eyed Mallesons from the hills heard their names and exploits from her smiling lips. Sanders Malleson, the piper, when he got his, nearly burst with pride. His eye flashed, he threw his head up; then he bowed deeply to her, turned and struck up the Austrian Anthem. He marched away with it as if he were plunging into battle. Helena stood where she was perched up on the dais and watched him with clasped hands. Her eyes filled with tears at the reckless finery of the noise. She was no Austrian, but the good chap didn't know that—and, of course, she knew that he didn't. It was the swagger and gallantry as much as the compliment which moved her.

The Baron, sitting his pony, took off his hat and watched everything from beneath frowning brows. I don't think he liked it. But he made a point of congratulating Pierpoint upon his triumphs.

IX

THE BALL

ALL this by way of prelude to the ball which followed it. That was Helena's day. There was nobody to touch her. She had been quiet at the Gathering, sedate while all the young men capered and ran about, as it were, for her approving smiles. And they got them, no doubt; but they all had their share. She gave them back all that they gave her. She had had herself well in hand that day, and there was no difficulty in calling her thirty at least. But at the ball she looked like a girl. She wore cloth of silver, cut rather narrow, and made very plainly. Her neck was bare of ornament. She had a snake—a flexible. snake—of silver in her hair; and I believe that was all. You didn't want jewels with eyes like hers. Hector got flowers for her, but she couldn't dance with flowers in her hand and soon discarded them. Her best flowers were in her cheeks. She was naturally a pale woman; but she was excited. That gave

her an exquisite flush.   There's a rose called
Madame de Watteville which comes nearest
to it.   She certainly was a lovely creature
that night— and she danced from the beginning to the very end of the end.

If it hadn't been for the Highland things—
reels and strathspeys—my poor friend would
have had no show; for Hector was no dancer.
You could see that by the look of him. He
held himself too stiffly; he was too serious;
if you understand me, he was too much the
gentleman for anything short of a *contredanse*
or a minuet. He would have tripped through
that I don't doubt. He was good at bowing,
and used to take his hat off as if he was going
into church when he met a lady. But I don't
think anything would have tempted him to
put his arm round a girl's waist—I mean, any
waist; and as for banging her about in the
ultra-modern way, he would sooner have gone
to hell—indeed, would have been there while
he was at that rude game. So he took the
reels in her company, and I caught sight of
them now and again—of him talking and of
her looking down at her silver toes while she
listened. She wasn't a great talker, but she

was an awfully good listener. She was one
of the women to whom men love to talk of
themselves. She chattered nonsense to the
boys like any girl, however—to Patrick and
some of his pert young friends. As for Pierpoint—well, personally, I was touched by her
excitement and complacency in his company.

I had one dance with her myself, about
midway through the first act—the before-
supper act—during which things were going
pretty well. I mean that the Marchioness
was there, with two of her girls, the Ladies
Rosalind and Alice, and that Pierpoint, who
was a great intimate at Dunmally, had done
something of his duty by them. Lady Larbert was a little, thin, upright woman with
very bright black eyes. She wore a tiara
better than anyone I ever saw, as if she had
every right to it—birth, purchase and air—
which she certainly had. She was noble, she
was rich, and very smart. She was so smart
that she had no need whatever for seeming
to be. So she never did. Even when she
wore her diamonds she didn't seem to know
it. She had her fancies—one of them was to
be bored at Inveroran; another was to be fond

of Pierpoint. She must have known what
he was, and she ought to have known that he
would never do for one of her girls—but she
risked that because she liked his good looks.

She didn't approve of Helena. I saw her
eyes glitter bleakly as the pretty creature
was switched about by our high-coloured
young friend. But she had no pique for
him; she put it all down to Helena's score,
and paid off part of it by striking up a great
friendship with the Baron. They hobnobbed
at considerable length in the anteroom, the
conservatory, and elsewhere, and I should
like to have overheard them, because the
Baron could be the very best of company
when he pleased. There was nothing local
about him. He was the perfect cosmopolitan.
I heard also afterwards—as I might have
supposed—that he knew at least two of her
boys, the one at Bucharest, the other in
Constantinople. He had probably met Dunmally, the eldest, in several places, proper
and improper.

But, on the whole, and with one unfortunate exception, there was no trouble until
the Larberts were off our hands.

My own dance with Helena was a revelation to me, though I had understood that Austrians could dance. It was like floating a rose-leaf, it was like steering a foam-bubble. She was exquisitely yet impalpably there; the leading spirit drawing you on, inexhaustible yet subservient. She inspired rather than led you. It was like the guidance of a spirit—the spirit of wingless flight. Wings would have been an offence to such motion as she evoked. You would have felt their beat, it would have jarred. Her motion was rather that of a stream of soft strong wind, filling space, and drawing you after it into finer and cleaner climes. She didn't talk, nor did I; she seemed not to breathe—and we didn't stop until the music had ceased to be. I was intoxicated and unwilling to leave her. At the moment I felt like drawing her out into the air, and on and on, over the world —to possess altogether this divinely rare being.

But we behaved after the human fashion, and talked as rationally as might be. I hope that she didn't see what she might have done with me at the time; and yet I'm not at all sure that she did not. I remember that she

9

pleaded with me like a child, as if excusing
herself for naughtiness.

"You don't like me—you don't approve oɪ
me. No—I feel it. But I'm happy, and you
ought not to mind that." This was heady talk.

"Did I know," she said, "that she hadn't
danced for seven and a half years?"

I didn't—and didn't quite believe it.

She assured me it was true. "He—my
husband—didn't like it after——"

She didn't finish. I said, "Then he won't
like me."

Her eyes were wide. "Oh, yes. He does
like you. He likes you very much. He doesn't
mind it here. He likes nearly everybody here."

"So do you, Baroness, I hope."

She sighed.

"Do you know," she said, "that I have been
breathing ever since I came to England.
Deep, deep breaths I have taken—to make up
what I have lost."

That was touching, and left me speechless;
but there was more to come. She looked
timidly at me. There was a humid brightness
in her eyes which should have warned me
that she was going to be unreserved.

"You won't misunderstand me? I shall
tell you what it is that I breathe. It is good-
will."

"Oh," I cried, "you will find oceans of
that."

"I do," she said, "and it is so good for me.
Do you know what I want more than everything in the world? It is to be liked by
people."

"Dear Baroness," I said, "everybody in
England will love you—" and there I was cut
off by Pierpoint, come to claim his share
in my promise.

I don't want to exaggerate— and it's not
at all necessary. I believe I am right in
stating that, after supper, Master Pierpoint
danced with her all the rest of the night. Of
course I wasn't there all the time—I was
dancing myself, as the business seemed, so to
speak, in the air. I was dancing, and I was
sitting out, and when I wasn't doing one of
those things I was smoking cigarettes in the
conservatory, which opens on to what they
call the East drawing-room. It used to be
Lady Mary's own room in her days. But
whenever I was dancing, Pierpoint was whirl-

ing Helena about; or if he wasn't doing that
he had her tucked away somewhere. That
was what led to trouble—a momentary
trouble. She was to have supped with the
grandees—but that's just what she didn't
do. Sir Roderick had intended to arm her
into that; but he couldn't find her; nor could
anybody else. My belief is that she had
supper in another part of the house altogether,
but I don't know it for a fact. There was
consequently some electricity about. It was
rather pink for a bit. When no one was
looking I abstracted her name-card, and with
the connivance of Miss Bacchus, friendly old
soul, bridged the gap. Lady Larbert glittered
like a frost.

Later on, of course, everybody noticed the
goings-on of the pair, and there was a good
deal of chattering among the resting couples.
Sir Roderick was cross, and, as usual on such
occasions, seemed to think it was done to hurt
his feelings. He was always like that. He
confided himself to Hector, I am sure. I saw
him puffing his cheeks, and spreading out his
chest; I caught, "Consideration for me, sir—
the commonest civility—" and guessed the

rest. But the Baron, as you may guess, never
turned a hair. He watched her, as he watched
everything; but he set his face harder than a
rock, and was always ready with his joke or
his elaborate bow. Did he feel that she was
slipping through his fingers? Ah, I don't
know.

I had thought her a tallish woman, and at
Gironeggio in particular I thought that she
looked every day of her age. In Pierpoint's
arms she looked to me like a slip of a girl,
so light that her little feet scarcely brushed
the floor. The top of her head reached his
collar, I suppose; her cheek lay against the
hollow of his shoulder. The other was
flushed and sleek. Her eyes looked heavy,
and she seldom raised them as he steered or
swirled her about. Being of the race she was,
you may be sure that she could dance—I
have told you what I thought of it; being of
the sort he was, you may be sure of him, too.
They made a brave show—and not a year's
difference between them, to look at them.
You couldn't expect a pretty woman not to
like that kind of thing. She liked it awfully.
. She drank it as her old Baron used to drink

cigar-smoke. And why on earth not, as Miss
Bacchus said. *She* couldn't drink cigar-
smoke—nor anything else: at any rate, she
never did drink anything but water. So why,
asked Miss Bacchus, shouldn't she drink
music and motion, and young men's homage,
and young men's breath? That's what she
asked me—and I couldn't answer her. "Hang
it, man," said the old virgin, "she's not
cattle. If *he* drinks, let her drink. That's
what I say." She said more—but I respect
my pen.

There would have been an explosion at the
end—saved by the Baron from being rather
serious. The Dunmally lot left after supper,
and other guests from outside began to go
away at about two in the morning. By three
or half past they were all away. But the
house-party kept it up. The last dance was
somewhere about five; and then we all had
coffee and buns, and, as Colonel Vane would
say, "By Gad, sir, we wanted it."
The cigarettes came round; the girls began
to smoke; Helena would not. She was very
still and rich with her escapade. I thought

her breathing showed that she was trying to recover herself. The Baron lit a cigar, and looked at her over the horrible dancing flame of his match. I thought he wanted to catch her eye; but he didn't.

Pierpoint got up and pulled the curtains back. Then he opened the window wide and looked out, whistling softly to himself.

He turned round with his fine face sparkling with devilry. "I say, it's a ripping night. Stars all over the place—some of them like lamps. There'll be a gorgeous sunrise. Who'll come with me up the Ben?"

There was a hush. I saw the Baron pull himself together. Patrick said, "I shall cleave to my brother." Another youth said, "Right-o," and looked at his late partner. They were all for it.

Pierpoint was looking at Helena, Hector was looking at her, so was her husband. Presently it came to pass that everybody was either looking at her, or waiting for what she would do. It was a "test case," said Miss Bacchus, perspicuous as usual.

She sat there, breathing deeply, looking down at her hand on the table. I know that

she wanted to go. I know that if she had
gone, there would have been a row. Hector
would have lost his temper. Sir Roderick
had lost his already.

The Baron said, "My friend, they want
you to go. The air will do you good."

It was brave of him. He did it very well
indeed. As for her, she looked at nobody but
Sir Roderick—neither at her husband, nor
Hector, nor at Pierpoint. To Sir Roderick
she said, "It would be delightful, but I am
too tired. As it is, I shall sleep forever."
Then she got up and smiled rather appeal-
ingly—still at Sir Roderick—"I shall say
good-night while it is still dark." And then
she went quietly away. It was as if she had
said, "I know I have been a naughty girl,
but you see how good I am trying to be now."

The Baron said, "So!" and resumed his
cigar. The young ones fidgeted about to see
what Pierpoint meant to do. Wynyard went
off to bed, and so did I, gladly. I believe that
the rest of them did the deed. Pierpoint in
the sulks went up exactly as he was—in
dancing pumps. He ought to have limped for
the rest of his leave, but he didn't.

X

SEQUELÆ

HECTOR was very unhappy, it was evident,
and I don't wonder. To be cut out by your
younger brother is not jolly; and when he
is so resplendently the better man in form
and favour, you have the desperate feeling
of the foregone conclusion to add to your
other troubles. It doesn't make things any
better to remind a man who is getting the
worst of the deal that he doesn't deserve anything better. Perhaps they *were* a pair of
rascals—though I don't admit it; but even
if they were, Hector was a gentleman. A
gentleman will fall in love with another man's
wife if he—well, if he does. He can't help
his feelings—or his tentacles, if you like.
It's when he *makes* love to such a lady that
the world calls him names, and—if he is unsuc-
cessful—opprobrious names. Hector would
have been very ready to meet the world on
its own ground. He abounded in theory and
loved an argument; but in this case I am

pretty sure that he had done no love-making
—unless you call his talks about the rights of
beauty love-making. It's a fine point that.
Now, as for Mr. Pierpoint, he was a pirate—
a freebooter, as you shall hear.

A day or two after the ball—on the day,
in fact, appointed for the von Broderodes'
departure, Miss Bacchus sought me out with
an air of mystery. She came into the library
where I was alone and peacefully at work.
and required me to walk with her. "I shall
be on the terrace," she said, and left me to
my conclusions.

When we were well away, on the river
walk, she said, "You are Hector's friend and
will do what you think proper. I've had
it out with her—no, that's wrong; she had
it out with me. She did it rather prettily.
She came and sat by me in the morning-
room, and after a bit put her hand on mine,
and spoke with her head on one side, as if
she was matching skeins. *You* know." I
did. "Presently she said, 'Miss Bacchus,
I should like you to talk to me a little. I
thought that you looked kind—I thought
so directly I saw you.' I told her that I was

the kindest old thing on two legs,
but no bite, for good people. 'I.
caught her. She said, 'I hope I am ͺ
I ought to be. I want to be.' And then ͺ
began and told me all about it. She's a good
girl, you know."

"Miss Bacchus," I said, "before *you* begin,
let me beg of you: no secrets of the bower."

"Gracious," said she. "Don't you be
afraid. You won't get any secrets out of me
—because there aren't any—or, if there are,
I don't know 'em. But I don't believe it.
You know Pierpoint every bit as well as I
do——"

"No," I said, "I don't believe I do. He's
no friend of mine—and couldn't be, since
I'm Hector's friend. As a matter of fact,
this time he's hardly exchanged a word with
me."

"I think he's a rogue," said Miss Bacchus;
"but she doesn't. She admits that he's made
a great impression on her. She says that
what makes it difficult is that her husband
seems to like him. Now, I don't understand
that."

"I do," I said. "He hates him like poison,

really, but he despises him. He knows that he could deal with the likes of Pierpoint. But he has a respect for Hector, who he thinks has done him a really bad turn. He hates Hector fundamentally—Pierpoint just on the surface. Pierpoint's a flea to him; Hector's a disease."

"Well," said Miss Bacchus, "you're taking me out of my depth. I don't know anything of psychology—never did. All I know is that Pierpoint kissed her the night of the ball."

"Well," I said, "I should think so."

"Just what I said to her," said Miss Bacchus. "'I'll warrant him,' I said. But she was very penitent."

"I like her for that," I said. "She's got a gentle heart."

"*Amor a cor gentile ratto s'apprende,*" said Miss Bacchus with aptness and elegance.

"I made little of it. 'Pooh!' I said, 'what's a kiss in a conservatory?' Then she was really rather funny, poor dear——"

"No secrets of the bower," I implored her, but she was inexorable with a good tale in her head.

"Helena said, 'No, I suppose not—but *one* was in the library.' I did my best, but she felt me shaking—and looked so unhappy that I gave her a kiss myself."

"That was kind of you," I said.

"Well," said Miss Bacchus, "damn it all, you know."

I thought myself that the story was a good one, but that two kisses admitted was rather a serious matter—from all points of view. It almost established a habit, it certainly established a precedent. Miss Bacchus took a more robust view.

"She's a very pretty woman," said she; "he'd been dancing with her all the evening —and there you are. I don't think there's much in it. But you must decide for yourself what you are going to say to Hector."

"Oh, Hector!" I said at once. "Poor chap, I shall say nothing at all, unless he speaks to me. Least said soonest mended. I need not assure you that I shall respect her confidence, since you have handed it on to me. I don't think you ought to have done it, to be candid with you. It shall go no further—I promise you that."

"Well, I should think not," said she. "I had my reasons for telling you—and I thought you were to be trusted."

"Your exquisite reason—" I demanded, and she told me.

"Von Broderode has asked Pierpoint out to his place in the winter—for shooting or hunting. He's going. Now Helena don't want him to come—or tells me so. But he's going, I believe. Can't you get Hector to go, too? That's what I want you to do."

I was startled. "My dear friend, how on earth am I to ask Hector to go and shoot with another man? You can hardly be serious."

"I assure you that I'm not a fool," she said. "Helena herself is going to ask Hector. She thinks—she's afraid—he will refuse to come."

"Well," I said, "after the way she has treated him——"

"I know," said Miss Bacchus. "That's what she feels, too. Now it's up to you to get him round. Don't frighten him, you know. Just wake him up."

I shook my head. "I *should* frighten him.

No, no. That won't do. She must ask him herself."

"I tell you she means to," said Miss Bacchus. I stopped our walk and spoke my mind. I said, "Look, here Miss Bacchus, this is pretty bad, you know. She's at least four years older than Pierpoint; and if he's a rogue, to say the least of it, she ought to know better. Hector's is another affair altogether. You know what he is. You know that he would never do her any harm. Well, now she ought to have met him more than half-way. If you ask me, I think that he'll be well out of it all. He's been wretched enough here—and it's her fault. No, no. I am for letting him get over it."

Miss Bacchus had been preparing herself for me while I was holding forth. I saw it in her fishy old eye. It was a cold, greenish, calculating eye—as flat as a snake's.

She said, "My fine man, your rhetoric has carried your wits away. That woman is a child at heart. She was married out of a convent to that old rake. God knows what he's done with her—and God only knows. But I know, and so do you, that he's kept

her to himself. I don't suppose she has
talked to a man for ten minutes alone since
she's been married. What have years got
to do with it? They may make a fool of her,
if you like—that's all the difference they'll
make. She'll go to the deuce, and the likes
of you will say she ought to have known
better. How on earth could she know? Don't
talk such nonsense. You ought to know Hector
better than I do. He's your friend, not
mine. But I'm as sure as I stand here that
Hector would rather be in the fire than let
her slip into trouble. And there's another
thing. So far as I can understand, it is he
who has brought her up to the edge of trouble.
Very well, then, the least he can do is to pull
her back again."

I had to confess that she was right.

The crisis was reached at luncheon. The
von Broderodes were leaving by the four
o'clock train. They were going on to the
Marquis's for a week on their way to London.
That had been understood. What was not
understood by the Baron was that Pierpoint
was going to the Marquis's, too.

During lunch von Broderode made a kind

of speech to Sir Roderick. It became a kind
of speech. "I am glad to have seen your
beautiful country under your care," he said.
"I believe that I have seen the most beautiful
part of it. Perhaps that is not fair to Scotland; but it is very good for me. I assure
you that I leave you painfully." Sir Roderick
crowed like a moor cock.

"My dear Baron, you must pay us another
visit. Now that you have found us out,
hey?"

The Baron twinkled and shone. "Yes, I
have found you out." He was looking full
at Pierpoint as he said it—he used a rich full
voice, with mockery in it—at least, it sounded
so to me. "I know what to expect of you.
The welcome Highlander, as you say." Patrick
kicked me under the table. "But before that
happens, you are coming to try your luck
in Galicia—ha?" This, of course, to Pierpoint
who said, "Thanks, yes. I should love it."

"That is good for all of us," said the Baron,
and looked all round the table. Then it was
that Helena, in clear tones, to be heard by
everybody, spoke to Hector.

"I hope very much that you will come
10

with your brother," she said. "You will be pleased with Galicia. I wish you to like it so much." She spoke studiedly, but with great courage. She was pale, but had very bright eyes.

I never saw the Baron put out before. He was angry this time. His nostrils opened wide. As for his eyes, they blazed. He said nothing at all, but looked straight at the man he believed his enemy. I was right and Miss Bacchus was wrong. It was Hector he feared.

He got over it in a moment, but he didn't back up his wife's move. Hector flushed deeply, and murmured that he should be most happy. I gathered from the way he said it that he didn't mean to go—and I don't wonder. But she might make him—she probably would. I felt sure that she would try.

After lunch is always a desultory sort of time. One loafs about and wants tea. But I saw that Helena got what she wanted— a *tête-à-tête* with Hector. Pierpoint had disappeared. They went off together over the lawn, and I had to imagine the rest. I am sure she meant to be kind to him.

And then they went. Pierpoint was not with them. But he had left Inveroran already, in his own trap. They seemed to think he would go directly to Dublin from Dunmally. His leave was nearly up.

That was the night of the servants' ball. I had two dances with Ethel Cook, the handsome housemaid. She was easily the queen of that party; none of our girls came near her, though Elspeth Muir was an uncommonly pretty girl.

Ethel Cook was dressed in grey, and had a red rose in her hair. She talked quite well, but was rather reserved. I said something about the day's departures, that it was a pity Mr. Pierpoint wasn't there. She said, with a dry voice, that he was better employed.

XI

THE FIRMNESS OF HECTOR

SHORTLY after these events I went South and got immersed in my departmental work and the mild relaxations of a London before Christmas. I had had no confidences from Hector. He did not choose to discuss his affairs, and I couldn't question him about them. I can't say that he was even normally cheerful. He was very gentle; but he was always that. On the other hand, he wasn't in the deeps of misery. He held his head up and did what his station up there required of him. Just as I was leaving he said that he should probably see me in London during the winter. I said that I should expect to put him up—he always came to me when he was in London—and he made no immediate answer. Then he said, "It's all in the air at present. We'll write about it." That was how it had to be left.

I went to London, I got busy, I saw nobody connected with the Mallesons, I forgot the

von Broderode comedy and all to do with it—
until one afternoon in November when I went
into my club.   There in the hall was old
Vane in the act to depart, with cigar in mouth
and match in hand.

We hardly know each other.   I nodded and
passed on to the hat-peg department.   But
he turned and called after me.   At the same
moment the match burned his finger.

"D—— the match," he said as I returned.
"Oh, I say, I wish you'd clear something up
for me.   It's about—" and here he began to
whisper—"it's about young Malleson—you
know the chap I mean.   Chap in the 16th——"

"Pierpoint?"   I was all there in a second.
"What's he been up to?"

The Colonel looked at me from under his
glasses with the intolerably supercilious effect
that trick always has—as if to say, 'What
kind of a silly ass might you be?'   Then he
seemed to give me up.

"Made sure you'd know.   Why, he's sent
in his papers.   That's what he's done."

I thought immediately of all that this might
mean.   "Are you sure about that?" was what
I said—to gain time.   It annoyed the Colonel.

"It's in the *Gazette*—if that's what you mean! Now, what's he been up to?" That was exactly my question to him of a minute ago.

I said, "I haven't heard from Hector ever since I left Inveroran. But I expect that I shall now. Pierpoint doesn't love me very much—and I've never given him any reason why he should."

"Oh," said the Colonel, "I think he's a rip. But they'll stand a lot of that kind of thing. But I'm sorry for the old chief—he's a fine old cock. This will make him moult a tail-feather or two—I'll be shot if it don't." I am sorry to add that he chuckeld rather snugly over the thought. "Devilish proud old boy is the chief. And Pierpoint the apple of his eye." With that comfortable reflection the Colonel grasped his umbrella firmly in the midst and stalked off with a curt salutation.

I was dead certain that this had something to do with Helena von Broderode, though why I thought so, or what it had to do with her, I couldn't tell you. And it was one of those sort of things you can't ask about for

fear of the worst. Hector was in my thoughts
—I was awfully fond of Hector in my own
way—I would have given anything to see
him. But there was nothing to be done:
I must wait for him, quite sure that sooner
or later he would see me about it. I don't
mind owning that for a week or more I slunk
about town as if I were under a cloud. I
saw Chevenix in Pall Mall one afternoon, and
fairly bolted up into St. James's Square. I
was careful where I dined, lest I should happen
upon Miss Bacchus. She would have raked
me fore and aft, I knew. I was virtually in
hiding: no private views, no first nights.
It was a bad time.

Finally, I had a line from Hector—but
that wasn't till mid-December. He wrote
very shortly: "I must be in London for a
few days before the feast. I hope very much
to see you. You can put me up for a night
or two, I'm sure. Don't ask anybody to
meet me.—H. M. M."

He came. He looked very serious; but
he was a proud chap and very sensitive, so
I let him have his head. I was dining out

the night he came, and returned at about eleven or half-past. He was sitting before the fire with a book and his pipe.

He began to talk with an effort—pure instinct on his part to avoid the unavoidable. As nearly as may be he said this:

"You know that Pierpoint has chucked the Army, of course."

I said that I had been told so. Had they known that he intended it?

"None of us knew it," he said, "until he wrote to my father. Personally, I wasn't surprised. You see, I know him."

"What did your father say?" I asked.

"He made out—or tried to make out—that he was very glad of it. He admitted that Pierpoint was his favourite. He said it would be a comfort to him to have him at home— and all that kind of thing. It was as plain as a pikestaff that he was awfully upset. He couldn't make it out at all."

"But," I said, "he didn't suspect anything awkward—any trouble?"

"No, I don't think he did. He thinks very highly of everything belonging to him. It would pretty well kill him. I hadn't the heart to try to prepare him—for anything, you know. I suppose I shall have to do something."

I said, "My dear fellow, I can see that you have faced it. Don't talk to me about it if you'd rather not. *Has* he got into a mess, do you think?"

"I don't think he has," he said. "But I think he intends to."

I was now pretty sure, not only that he did, but in what direction his mess was to lie; but I said nothing at the moment. I waited for Hector, who sat up before me like a bronze, burrowing deeply into his own recesses.

He broke out in such an unexpected place that I gasped.

"My father doesn't like her, you know," he said. "That's the worst of it." This was absurd. Sir Roderick liked everybody who liked him; and that Helena liked him was as plain as my cook.

I cast my hesitations to the four winds. "My dear Hector," I said, "you don't contemplate—you can't contemplate a catastrophe without stirring from your place!"

He said with perfect gravity, "I don't see what I can do."

He was difficult to deal with in this impassive mood. He seemed to be in another world, breathing an alien air, subject to an alien code of morals. But I was annoyed.

"Do, my dear chap!" I cried. "You can do all sorts of things—and nobody else can do anything. Do you sit there and tell me that you intend to let Pierpoint go out to Galicia alone?"

He didn't move a muscle. "I am not going with him, if that is what you mean."

He frightened me. I thought he was out of his mind. And after that I was doubly annoyed, because he was so infernally sane about it.

"Very well," I said. "It's your affair, and not mine. You have to reflect upon your responsibilities, how far you may have been concerned in bringing this about. I won't say any more. And you will do me the justice to remark that I have said nothing throughout unless you have invited me."

He softened at once, and became more human. "I know, I know. You have been very good about it. You were in it from the beginning, and have had every reason to take an interest. And you are the best friend I have. I know that very well. But this is how I feel about it. I hope you'll understand me. You and I aren't in agreement—as to the rudiments, I mean. We differ in first principles. Therefore, if I have made up my mind upon my course of conduct, I've made it up, you see, on premises which you dispute. So there's no common ground for us. I say this so that you may leave off being offended with me. I *must* do what I think right. That, at least, you will agree to."

Naturally, I agreed to it, and most certainly I didn't want to dig up the whole thing from the foundations and discuss the ground plan. But I thought I might as well find out exactly what he thought was going to happen—and asked him plainly, Did he suppose Pierpoint and she had come to an understanding?

He said that he did suppose so, though he *knew* nothing. "I haven't spoken to Pierpoint—indeed, I haven't seen him since he left us to go to Dunmally."

"Then you infer it from his chucking the service?"

He nodded to that.

"Then," I said, "you must also suppose that he and she are going to do a bolt."

He said, "I do suppose so."

I must say he took it cooly for a lover. But you never know with these emotional men what they are doing beneath their externals. I made one more effort.

"It is easy to see," I said, "that if you were with him you could prevent that."

He still stared at the fire.

"Why should I prevent it?" he said. "She wouldn't come with me."

"I hope you wouldn't ask her to," I said; "in fact, I am sure you wouldn't."

He looked quickly at me. "Oh, but you are wrong. I should decidedly ask her if I thought that she cared about me. But she doesn't—not in that sort of way."

"That being so, my dear Hector," I said, "she had much better stay where she is That seems to me self-evident. I don't see how the most extreme idealist could wish a woman to be carried off by a man four years younger than she is, still less when that man is your brother Pierpoint, of whose conduct

and conversation you are a better judge than
I am."

"Anything," said Hector, "is better for
her than remaining with that dying Priapus,
who only lives so long as she has any vitality
in her."

There was a dreadful certainty about him
which baffled my speech. I was prepared
for a high line, but not for such lengths of
fanaticism.

It was difficult to argue with a man like
that; and of course he knew more about
Helena than I did. To anybody but Hector
I should have said that she had plenty of
ways of protecting herself. She wasn't a
girl, she wasn't a fool. She might refuse to
live with him—anything in the world would
be better than what he contemplated for her
with such gloomy complacency, if I may say
that.

But I didn't feel that I could go on with
that sort of wrangle. It always made me
angry to be stone-walled. So I said—what
I was far from believing—that it was by no
means certain that she would be persuaded
by Pierpoint. She was a Catholic, she was

a mother, she seemed a God-fearing, or at least a world-fearing, woman. I said that she struck me as a cold nature. Heaven help me! Suppose he had known what Miss Bacchus knew, for instance.

Perhaps he did, for he stopped me, saying, "You are wrong. She has not a cold temperament. She is enthusiastic, and quickly moved." Then he said quickly and fervently, with a break now and then in his voice, "I love her with all my soul. She is my ideal of what a woman should be—ardent, devoted, yielding, gentle, and kind. She could not do an unkind thing; but if she were deeply moved she could do any daring thing. I would gladly have braved the hard eyes of the world, the shooting tongues, the cruel, pointing fingers—to serve her! But I have never spoken to her of my hope. Now—if she is so blessed as to have a heart full of love— if she is so blessed—let her go with him in God's name. It will give me a right to stand by her. She will be my sister, and shall have a brother's love from me. If one no else will save her from her captor I will."

"Save her, by all means," I said. "But

you will have to save her from Pierpoint by
and by."

"I know that," he said. "Pierpoint will
want to be off."

"You are allowing her to get into an intolerable position," I told him. "You don't
know what you are doing."

He said, "She is in an intolerable position
already. There is no other way of saving
her."

I said, "Hector, I urge you to go out there
—either at once or when he goes."

He showed me cavernous eyes—cavernous
eyes with despair in the depths of them.
"I can't go—I can't go," he said. "I love
her too much. It would tear my heart to
pieces."

We talked on, I suppose, half the night;
but it was only a going over the ground again.
Once more at least I brought him up to the
point where it seemed a matter of that or
nothing. Once more, when fairly up against
it, he broke back and said that he couldn't.
No man wants to see the woman he loves
elope with another man; no man wants to
lay himself open to such a taunt as Pierpoint

baulked might have against him. Pierpoint
might say, You profess to love this woman;
you know that she loves me. Yet you leave
her with a man abhorrent, whom you have
taught her to abhor; you are content to do
that sooner than see her happy with anybody
but yourself. Pierpoint might say that.
Hector may have felt its force. My belief
is that Hector had taught himself to want
her to elope. He had made a monster out
of the Baron. As for himself, I don't think
he thought of himself. That's where he was
so inhuman.

   The rest of his conversation with me during
the few days he was at my place may be
summarized thus: he had no conversation
with me. It is literally true. The morning
after that which I have recorded he was very
silent. When I came back in the evening
he had recovered somewhat. We dined at
the club, looked in at a theatre, chatted
desultorily, and went to bed. Next day he
was out to dinner somewhere. The day after
that he went away, having received a telegram. I believe it was from Pierpoint; but
he didn't tell me. He went away without a

word to me about Helena. I couldn't say anything, or do anything. He didn't mean me to.

Having done my little best and been
snubbed for it, I washed my hands of poor
old Hector's family affairs, and now felt at
liberty to go out into the world. The world,
as I might have known, if I hadn't been so
self-conscious, persisted in rolling on. Pretty
women still went to the tea-shop of the
moment with very young or very old gentlemen in attendance; Parliament still talked
about Home Rule; the *National Review* still
·asked us to take its word for it that Ministers
were common pickpockets, and still we didn't.
Christmas came round, and we all went
away. There were two days' skating and
thirty days of rain. At the end of January,
just as I was saying to myself that in two
months more I might get down into Provence,
with the wind, I met Miss Bacchus at a party
and took her down to dinner. On the stairs
she said to me, "I suppose you know all
about it."

I did, then. "Do you mean the best or
the worst?" I said.

11

"Oh," said she, "it all depends. I believe Hector thinks it's capital."

"Then," I said, "he's done it."

"Who has done what?" she said, evidently not sure whether I knew anything or not.

"Why, Apollo," I said. She was satisfied. "I'll tell you presently," she concluded— and then we were at table.

"All I know is," she said, "that Pierpoint has written to his father. I know that from Elspeth Muir, who was there when the letter came. She said the old man nearly had a fit."

I stopped her there. "Look here," I said, "do let us have one thing clear first. What did Pierpoint say in his letter?"

She didn't know. Of course she didn't.

"Very well," I said. "Then what did the chief say in his fit?"

Again she didn't know. It was all a wild surmise. "The Marks were in the house. Hector was sent for. He's up there now. They sent all the outsiders away. I saw Lord Mark on Sunday."

"And what did Lord Mark tell you?" I wanted to know.

"Well, he said that Pierpoint was going to take her away."

I told her that I didn't believe it; but in my heart's core, knowing Pierpoint, I shivered. "At any rate," I added, "if Pierpoint *was* going to run away with her, he'd hardly tell his father about it—would he?"

She allowed that; but she thought that, without letting the cat out of the bag himself, he might have left the key about.

"Does Hector know—or suspect?" I asked her.

"They all know what there is to know," she replied. "It's a bad look-out for fair Helena."

I said, "She ought to have known better. Upon my word—a woman of her age."

"If she had been *his* age," said Miss Bacchus very acutely, "she *would* have known better."

XII

HELENA FLIES

IN that parlous condition I had to leave my
friend's affairs—his heart seething and bob-
bing, as it were, like a pippin in a brew.
Although I cursed Hector for a besotted
idealist who didn't think people went to the
devil so long as they went *his* way there—
I didn't feel that I could write and tell him so,
satisfaction as that would have been to myself.
I was so angry with him that I didn't remember how often I had been angry with him
before—nor even what superhuman luck he
had had more than once before. There things
had to remain, and there I left them, subject
to occasional stabs of consciousness when I
realised that, at the hour it was, Helena
might be a runaway wife, already rueing the
bad exchange she had made.

Then—some time in March, as I suppose—
Wynyard came to see me, appearing as if
shot out of the blue sky—Wynyard the lean
and grim and red, Wynyard the parody of

Pierpoint, astonishing by his likeness and unlikeness to his twin. Wynyard himself stalked into my rooms when I was at breakfast, nodded a curt good morning and asked, or looked, for food.

He had it, and consumed it in silence, or nearly in silence. All his comment was upon its excellence. "Awfully good bacon. There's a thing you simply don't *see* abroad. As for their coffee—muck." So he had been abroad! That was rare for him. But I knew him, and left him alone.

When he had really done, and had lighted his pipe, he gave me a shock. "Well," he said, "I thought you'd be interested to know . . . . I've cooked his goose for him."

"Whose goose, my dear chap?" I asked, though I guessed.

He said, "My beautiful brother's. He was going off with her. On the very brink."

"Well?"

"Well," said Wynyard, with narrowed eyes, "he won't."

"Oh," I said. "Are you sure?"

"I'm as sure," he said, "as that I've had breakfast."

I jumped to the thought of fair Helena.
"And what does she think about it? How
did she cool off? Because you have to blow
pretty hot to get such a tone in the air as the
elopement tone. . . ."

"I can't tell you," Wynyard said, "what
she thinks about it, because I don't know.
But I do know that Pierpoint is in Paris,
while she, I believe, is in Bucharest, or some
such place, with a Princess Glinka, a fat
woman who wants washing."

There was really nothing to say. If you
were to see a miracle there would be nothing
to say. That is the test of a miracle.

What I *did* say shows how little there was
to say. It was feeble, but it served.

"How do you know," I said, "that she
wants washing?"

"Because I've seen her," he replied. "She
was about—very much about. A great friend
of Helena's, and a good sort. A fat Roumanian who lives about, mostly smoking. I
had a talk with her. I told her she must stop
it. I said it was out of the question. She
lifted her fat hands and made tragic eyes—
at the ceiling, not at me. When she said,

'It is never out of the question for women
to fall in love,' I said, 'It is in this case.'
And I made her see it."

"Good Lord!" That was all there was to
say. Then I asked him how Pierpoint took it.

"Oh, Pierpoint didn't like it at all. I rather
shook Pierpoint. But there was nothing to
say. He's in Paris. I daresay he'll go after
her again after a bit. But Glinka will let
me know."

"Why did Glinka, as you call her, propose
to allow Helena to go at all?" That was
my next.

Wynyard told me, "Because Helena would
have gone without leave if she hadn't got it.
She was mad to go. She'd have gone with
Pierpoint sooner than not go."

So she had gone, then? Wynyard said, of
course she had gone. With Glinka, and for
the moment to Bucharest. She had made up
her mind, he said, to go before she left Inveroran last year. I wondered.

"Do you mean to say that she——?"

"No," he said. "I don't. She didn't tell
me. But I knew it."

This cold-eyed, hot-faced child of nature saw

more than one gave him credit for. But he
was always a shrouded creature. He had the
gift of silence.

"Did you say anything at all to Helena?
Did you talk to her?"

He stared. "Of course I talked to her.
She asked me to come and see her—at Bucharest. She took me to the convent to see her
daughter. A nice child."

"And has she run away with Hermione,
too?"

"No. Hermione stays where she is. She's
all right there."

I asked him, "How did she take Pierpoint's
defection, Wynyard? And what on earth
could he have said to her?"

Wynyard shrugged.

"God knows what he said. That wasn't my
business. As for her, she never mentioned
his name once. He might not have existed."

I understood that. She was a proud woman,
and would sooner have died. But would she
ever forgive him?

I turned to other points.

"What will the Baron do? Has she told
him, do you know?"

"She wrote to the Baron before she left."

"What will he do?"

Wynyard considered. "I think he'll get her back. The Baron's a man, or the remains of one. Personally, I like him."

"So do I," I said. Then I asked more about Pierpoint. He said that he didn't expect Pierpoint home for a bit. Pierpoint had thrown up his job, and as he had done it for nothing it was unlikely he would come home to explain it away. His belief was that Pierpoint would go after Helena.

"And if he does?" I asked. My own belief was that if he did, she would know how to deal with him; but Wynyard apparently thought it possible that she would not.

"If he does," said Wynyard, "I suppose that I shall go after Pierpoint."

"There'll be bloodshed," I told him.

"No, there won't," said Wynyard.

He went North that night, to console his father. I took the trouble to spread the good news about London. I told Miss Bacchus, who sniffed; I told Lord Mark, who snorted. "Wynyard's in love with her himself. They all are. The chief's in love with her. So are you. I call it rot."

I said, "I admit it. She's divinely pretty, and as soft as a bird's breast."

"Bah," said Lord Mark. "Give me a leathery woman." Somebody had.

The erring pair—I mean, of course, the Glinka and the fair runaway—went first to Castellammare, thence to Sicily, then to Corfù; from each of which sanctuaries in turn they were routed by German hordes whom Helena, poor girl, either knew or thought she knew, or suspected of knowledge. I can well imagine that the woods may have been full of eyes, that the Baron, so to speak,

Formosam resonare docuit Amaryllida silvas

—if I may make Virgil limp after me. He was not a man to be trifled with; nor could I judge him a man to let trifles of delicacy stand in his way.

Whether he pursued or not, they at any rate fled, believing in pursuit. And the Glinka was not made for a beast of chase. Although she was timorous, she was fat and loved her ease. She must have been very cross, and I can imagine that there may have been times when Helena almost regretted her servitude to her Baron's whim. I don't know the details of their flight, or by what stages they reached Tripolitza in Arcadia. They were there by the middle of June; and then they moved on to Sparta, or rather to Mistra, which is a romantic shell of a mediæval fortress-town upon the slopes of Taygetus. They were found there by Hector, who went out to visit them in October, and came back to London full of content with what he had seen and been told.

He said that they were installed in a convent, which was shared also by the priest and his family. A very domestic couple, he reported them: the Princess, black-browed, heavy, dusty, a smoker of cigarettes and eater of oranges; very fond of Helena, petting her more than she scolded, though she did that too. She had a tragic air, a deep bass voice, and was not beardless. Helena, he said, was softly beautiful and learning Greek from the priest, a mild-eyed, melancholy lotus-eater whose ways were soothing to her. Pierpoint —she had admitted the renegade!—had been with them in Athens, but Hector gave me to understand that Athens was made impossible for him—and that his hostesses left in a hurry. The Glinka, who hated Pierpoint, feared the Baron as much as cold water, or any water. It was she who insisted on bundling off, though she was the last person in the world to bundle. Not that the Baron had been there—no, but he had been heard of. He had certainly been in Greece and had left spies behind him. They were persons, Hector said, whom Helena knew. They did not speak to her, they did not even seem to be aware of her; but they haunted her. She sent Pierpoint away—but to no purpose. It became a silent persecution and gave her a bad attack of nerves. She limbered up her Glinka—or was limbered up herself—and moved by night, first to Patras, then to Tripolitza by carriage—heavy work for a sultry Roumanian princess who did not as a rule put on her clothes till four in the afternoon. But the peace and solitude of the mountain stronghold revived her wonderfully, and Hector believed that if the supply of French novels held out the Glinka would be content to remain through the winter. After that he didn't know what would happen.

He was on his way North, when he told me all this—to see his father and reassure him about Pierpoint. He himself seemed quite at ease. His heart was fixed, he said. His lady was free, knew that she was loved, accepted his devotion, and relied upon it. He was to hold himself ready to go to her at a moment's warning. I never met a lover of his sort before—a vicarious lover, a kind of carpet Cyrano de Bergerac. His ideas of romantic enchantment were too bleak for me.

"You think she is happy?" I asked him, and he replied at once that he did.

"Of course," he said, "she regrets the child. She has news of her from a friend whom she can trust. But, unfortunately—I rather gather this—she gets news about von Broderode too. That's a great bore—but it can't be helped."

"She has heard nothing from the Baron directly?"

He shook his head. "Not a word."

"She has written to him?"

"She wrote when she left him. She hasn't written since."

"You have no idea what he is doing?"

"Not the least, beyond what I have told you. I feel sure that he is not sitting still."

So did I.

He changed the subject of his own accord by saying that it was beautiful to see her so happy. "You would hardly know her again," he told me. "There is a light upon her which you never saw there—a saliency in her motions which is enchanting. And she has had a wonderful effect upon Pierpoint. He adores her, and gives no trouble at all. He's never been serious before: he's serious now. I don't believe that he has a care in the world."

It was quite obvious to me now that my poor Hector had no notion of Wynyard's share in·the game, and put down Pierpoint's withdrawal to innate virtue. Well, I let it go at that. But Helena's forgiveness of him could only be put down to one of two things: either she was excessively enamoured or he had lied enormously about his reasons.

I said that it seemed to me a great pity that Pierpoint should have been there at all, considering what he had proposed. Hector held his head very high, said that to suspect

her was to condemn myself; that Pierpoint
had been there because he loved her—"just as
I was myself," he added, with a fatuity only
possible to an idealist, and a Hector Malleson.
He was quite *sui generis* in that kind of saying.
He added afterwards that Helena was taking
her responsibilities very seriously.

I said, "That's an odd way of showing
seriousness." But Hector said, not at all.
"Pierpoint has no cares, because nothing is
difficult for him. She has called out his latent
ability. She has made him ambitious. I
am prepared to think rather highly of him."

I said, "He's not been tried yet. You should
wait till the Baron puts the screw on." Then
I noticed that Hector was prepared to make
a family matter of it.

"We shall be ready for him if he does anything offensive," said my remarkable friend.
"At present I don't see what he *can* do."

I pointed out one thing immediately, which
was that the Baron, having made Athens too
hot for Pierpoint, might make Sparta too
cold for his wife—by practically keeping her
there, alone with a bored Roumanian lady of
unsociable habits. I didn't know it, but I

was prophesying. Hector was wired for while he was at Inveroran—while I was there too. He showed me the telegram, which simply said—according to a code which they had arranged beforehand—"Leaguer"—and off he went.

After a fortnight we heard from him—or from *them*, rather. I had a letter from Hector, which said, "The Baron is at the hotel at Sparta. She was sketching in Mistra when he was carried up the street in a kind of swinging chair—with a guide to point him out the objects of interest. She, poor child, sat frozen in her place, not daring to look at him. He took his hat off, and was carried on. Since that time he has installed himself at Sparta, within easy distance of her. He has Teresa Visconti, his attendant, with him, a doctor, and a succession of friends. She cannot stop here, and the Princess will not. What to do I don't know at present. She has written to my father, with my full approval. If he speaks about it, I rely upon your friendship." That was all.

Well, she had indeed written to Sir Roderick. She had, it is simpler to say at once, cast her-

self into his bosom. That, whether a ruse or
an artless rush for safety, was the way to do
it. I never saw the old man so moved by
anything. He called us together—those of
us who were his familiars. We held a council
of war. He said that a beautiful and perse-
cuted lady had appealed to him for protection.
She and her husband had both been his guests,
and could claim equal rights from him. It
was no part of his business (he meant *our*
business) to judge between a husband and
wife. We might have our prejudices, they
might or might not be reasonable, or even
honourable. The thing was done: the lady
had left him. He, with no legal right to
support him, not asserting any such right,
chose to obtrude himself upon her, to beset
her. The lady, not knowing where to turn,
had written to him a noble, touching, affecting
letter, he said—he had it in his hand, tried
to read extracts from it, and broke down—
which no man of honour or common charity
could receive and not be affected by. He
said that there was but one thing to do—
namely, to offer her instant and unconditional
asylum. Inveroran, himself, his sons, his

12

friends were at her service. He had not called
us to advise him; he knew us too well to
doubt what our advice would be; we, he
believed, knew him too well to suppose him
in need of it. Hector would escort her. He
had telegraphed to Hector to that effect. He
ended up by saying that he was a proud man
that day. And he looked it.

We weren't a very big party that year.
The chief's audience consisted of Lord Mark,
Wynyard, Patrick, and myself. The first
named was the only one who said anything.
Wynyard squared his jaw, Patrick shuffled
his feet about and had his cheeks buried in
his hands. But Lord Mark said, that was
all right—very right and proper; but what
were we going to do about the neighbourhood?
People would talk, he said; and they didn't
like runaway wives in Scotland. The old
chief glared at him and asked him what he
meant. He wasn't at all dismayed. He said
he meant exactly what he said. They didn't
like wives who ran away. There were the
Larberts at Dunmally, for instance. Well,
they know everyone. One of the sons was in
the Ottoman Bank at Constantinople, for

instance. Now, suppose old Broderode came
across *him?* Well, the first thing that would
happen would be that the Dunmally people
would come over here with old Broderode's
story at their fingers' ends. The second
thing might be that old Broderode would be
asked to stay with them. We remembered
what went on at the ball up here! The
Marchioness was all for the Baron, and didn't
care a bit for Helena's goings on. Well,
what about that? So said Lord Mark in his
tone of querulous commonsense; and it was
not much help that Sir Roderick fumed and
glared at him. Wynyard took him as well as
it could be done, I believe. He said, "Very
well. Let them have him. He won't come
here, and that's all she cares about." Mark
said there'd be a beastly scandal—and Sir
Roderick jumped down his throat. A scandal
at Inveroran—raised by the Larberts—in Malleson country! Did Mark know what he was
saying? Mark, who did, perfectly well, subsided into sniffs and grunts, and the storm
died down; but afterwards he told me what
of course was in his mind. Pierpoint was
involved in this. Pierpoint had done his best

to elope with Helena. The Baron knew all
about that—trust him. Well, then, if the
Larberts got to know that, and then found
Pierpoint lodged in the house—with Helena
—well, said Mark, there'd be the deuce's own
fuss, and he didn't mind telling me that Lady
Mark wouldn't stand it. She was an American. "They call her stodgy," he said, "and
she may be stodgy—but she won't stand any
hanky-panky with the Seventh Command-
ment; and my position here will be devilish
awkward. I don't know what I shall do if
that woman comes here. My wife'll go to
America—that's certain. And I suppose she'll
stop there, because she won't come here while
the woman's in the house. And mark you
this"—he slapped the palm of one hand with
the finger of the other—"If she comes here,
she comes for good. That's a certainty."

He glared at me through his monocle, pausing for the reply which he didn't get. "Very
well," said he, "what happens then? Why,
you practically divorce me and my wife.
That's what you do. And that's what I call
chucking stones into a pond. You make rings.
you know. And it's *my* pond, I'll trouble

you." There was a good deal in what he said. though it wasn't clearly expressed.

But Lord Mark was the only malcontent. As for the rest of us, it seemed that the chief was on our minds and consciences, and we in a conspiracy to make what was not appear as if it was. I believe that with Helena's letter he took Helena herself to his heart. He talked of her as if she were daughter of the house. It was "When that child comes," or even "When that child comes back." Back! Now there never had been a daughter of the house. Not only had his wife given him no girl, but no Malleson chieftainess had had a daughter for several generations. It was odd, but so it was. The legend explained it, to the Malleson mind, the legend of Euphemia Grant and the Malleson curse—the Malleson malison, Pat used to call it. Euphemia had been a lady who loved too well. Since the day of her expulsion from Inveroran, it was said, there had never been a daughter to the house. So there was cause enough for Sir Roderick to take this willing lady to his bosom, or (since she had come there by the post) to keep her in it. In his own simple transparent way he was as much of an idealist as Hector. That which he desired to be, *was*. And so we all played up.

In the air—I don't know how to describe it, but was conscious of it for the three weeks I put in at Inveroran—there was a kind of suspense—a kind of vibratory feeling, as if the whole place was singing with preparation. It was exciting enough. Sandars felt it, I know, the careworn butler, who had begun as a bootboy when Sir Roderick had been put into his first kilt, and had climbed up to his present place. He was five years older than his master. I came down one day before anybody, and found him in distressful circumstances. Ethel Cook, that fine, tall housemaid, was before him, wiping her eyes with her apron. Sandars had his hand on her shoulder. "I could not do it, my girl, I could not——" There he broke off; but I had got away.

Another time I saw him crossing the hall with the kettle for tea, tiptoeing in his usual circumspect fashion. And yet he seemed to be labouring like a ship in the trough of a heavy sea. Then I saw him put the kettle down and cover his eyes with his hand. He

lifted his face towards the ceiling, and kept it
so, covered still. Then he shook his head
slowly, resumed his burden and went on his
way. I knew him so well that it was an
impulse hard to resist, to run after him and
ask what was the matter. I did resist it,
however, obeying that strange instinct of all of
us in that house to put the thing away from us,
and for the chief's sake pretend it wasn't there.

I renewed acquaintance with Ethel Cook at
the servants' ball; but she seemed to have
lead in her toes, and stopped after a couple of
turns. We were, of course, pretty old friends.
She had been six years at Inveroran. I
reminded her that she had been keener on
dancing last year, and she admitted it with
a sigh. She said, "Yes, but that was a year
ago. A deal has happened since."

I said, no troubles at home, I hoped. No,
she said, they were all well at home. She
hadn't been very well. I said—a change.
But she seemed to think that impossible.
"Oh, no, I couldn't go now——" and then
she stopped, as if she had said too much. An
electric condition of affairs—which gets on
the nerves of a household.

XIII

ASYLUM

Nothing happened until the spring, however.
When I left Inveroran in October Hector was
expected back during the next month. He
had escorted his two ladies to Paris, taking
Vienna on the way, where Helena had paid
a hidden visit to the child and pushed on.
The dusky Princess longed for the rue de la
Paix and wouldn't stop long. Besides, she
was terrified of the Baron.

When they reached safety in Paris Hector
thought it his duty to leave—and, in fact did
leave, it being understood that Helena should
come to Inveroran in May. He didn't mention Pierpoint to me when I saw him on his
way home; but I have reason to believe that
the amorist was in Paris too, and a good deal
in Helena's company. He was certainly there
in the spring when Hector went out to escort
the lady northwards, because she arrived,
like a captive Briseis, between the pair of
them.

184

I met them at Charing Cross one bright
afternoon in early May, and was immediately
struck by her soft and rich allure. She looked
eight-and-twenty, and amazingly pretty. She
had more colour; her eyes were brighter; she
was more vivacious. Love suited her. She
was like the burnished dove of the poem,
having a livelier iris. I thought Pierpoint
improved by his moustache and beard. He
looked more like his wholesome twin. As for
Hector, there was a kind of 'Bless you, my
children!' air upon him which gave me a fit of
chuckling whenever I looked upon his beaming paternal eyes. Nothing of the ousted
pretendant about him. Bless you, no! You
would have said that he had attained the
utmost of his desire.

I was not alone to receive them. Miss
Bacchus was there, by arrangement it seemed.
"Yes, I'm an accomplice," she told me. "I
don't know what you're all going to do with
her when the Baron dies. It will be an
unseemly scramble, I'm thinking—like the
end of the Austrian Empire. Personally, I
shall back the best man."

"Who's he?" I asked her. She said

"Well, the Baron will win—if he lives. That's a certainty."

I said that Inveroran was a long way off his beat. She nodded her head many times and said so had Sparta been. "These foot-in-the-grave people," she said, "live from point to point. You'll see." I did see; but at the moment I didn't believe her.

It was the chief, she told me, who had urged her to be hospitable to Helena, in a long letter. "He don't disguise his feelings," she said, "and has no need to. They do him great credit. Imagine an old autocrat of his age working out the details of a lady's visit to London! He's up to the neck."

"He wants a daughter," I said.

She said, "Hum!"

If Helena was pleased to see me—and I believe that she was—she was enormously relieved to see the old gentlewoman. It saved her from the odd look of being escorted by three men. I knew a girl once—a very popular girl—who was escorted home from a dance by forty men; but that was in Germany, where people are enthusiastic.

Helena clasped my hand warmly and said

how nice it all was, but she fairly jumped
at Miss Bacchus and hugged her to her heart.
"Oh, you kind, good creature. You are a
true friend! How could I ever know that the
English were so kind?"

I asked her, Hadn't Inveroran taught her
anything? She went on hugging Miss Bacchus
as she said, Everything! Everything! It
certainly had taught her a thing or two, as
they say.

I now had time to notice how triumphant
Hector showed up. As I said, it was as if he
had achieved the ambition of a lifetime. In
fact, as Miss Bacchus observed to me afterwards, he was the perfect uncle, for not only
must he fuss about the luggage and produce
the chit for the Custom House out of his
waistcoat pocket, but there sat visibly upon
him that air of having done something, pulled
something off which benevolent uncles always
have. Pierpoint seemed sheepish beside him
—the self-conscious nephew—as if he had
been found out in an enthusiasm by his
school-fellows. I don't know how far he
thought us all ignorant of his late fiasco: of
course he saw through Hector. Hector, good

ass, thought he had been called back at the last minute by his nobler nature. Helena knew what he had told her, too. But what about me? What about Miss Bacchus? It was on our score that he poked his head, I think, and looked like a flagging dog.

Helena, who had brought no maid with her, stayed with Miss Bacchus; and the lot of us dined with her that night. The old virgin had a flat in Kensington—in and out of which, so long as we were in London, Helena lived and moved. Poor girl, she never seemed at ease without the old friendly soul. She by no means had the Mallesons to dine every night. Hector saw her every day; but Pierpoint seemed very detached. He went to the races, and paid week-end visits. She wouldn't go anywhere in public with *him*—though she let me take her to the Academy, and Hector had her to himself at the Zoo. We had a box for *Tristan* at the Opera, and all went to that; but she was so much upset by the second act that she had to go out. Miss Bacchus went with her and left the three of us *plantés là.* Hector and I stayed it out. Pierpoint went off to the Empire. Helena was in an emotional

state, poor dear, always hovering between
tears of shame and tears of pure joy. She
could rarely trust herself to speak of her
reception by "the family," as she called us—
when she didn't lump us all together as "the
English." Mrs. Jack Chevenix came to call
upon her, and brought with her a quiet,
beautiful woman, a friend of hers, a Mrs.
Senhouse. Helena was deeply gratified by
that. She admired our countrywomen; she
said that they were a great testimony to the
voluntary system. On the same grounds she
supported the army. "They stand of themselves, your women," she said. "They choose
to do what we are forced to do. I think it
beautiful to see their proud bent heads. They
are like the Caryatides of the Erechtheum.
Women in Germany are drudges. And as for
the army—it is a herd." That was her view,
and what has happened since, and is still
happening, shows her acumen.

Then, towards the last week in May—with
Miss Bacchus as ballast—we all went up to
Inveroran. We took the boat from Glasgow,
ran down the Clyde in fog and rain, but got

into beautiful weather as we neared the islands,
and opened the bay upon as beautiful a morning as I remember to have seen. The air
seemed shot with blue and gold. There was
the sandy shore ahead of us, backed by mountain and cloud; the little white town; the
fishing-smacks tossing in the sparkling water;
there was the castle, with the flag streaming
out in the breeze of the upper air. A perfect
day.

She stood on the foredeck with her hand on
Hector's arm. A long motor veil, which she
had twisted up in her hair, flagged out like a
pennon. She had been up with the light,
waiting for this. So simple, so innocent, so
true—it seemed impossible to think ill of her!
And I know that I didn't—and yet—and yet
—I felt the intolerable pity of the thought that
but for a very little she might have been as
happy as she seemed. Everything was right
but one thing. She was one of those women
who simply must make a love-match. And
that was just what she couldn't do. Well, it
was no good thinking of it then. We were
practically there: the thing was to make the
best of it.

I made out the old chief in his kilt, with his
long walking-staff, from half a mile away. He
was alone, it seemed—and, thank the Lord,
there were no pipers in attendance and he had
come down in the motor instead of the state
carriage.

He was very shaky, very agitated, and so,
of course, was she. He took off his bonnet
when she came, and kissed her hand with
great formality. She wanted to refuse it but
didn't. He shook hands with Pierpoint,
silently, not trusting himself with words,
then with the rest of us. Hector went off
with the servant to look after luggage, and
told us not to wait for him. We all got into
the motor—Pierpoint in front, the two ladies
and the chief on the back seat. I was *vis-à-vis*.
Miss Bacchus and I did the chattering. I
saw that he had Helena's hand in his own·
Passing Rosemount, the empty white house
with its blank red blinds, I had a momentary
shiver, remembering the Baron's fierce trans-
ports of a year and a half ago. But I felt all
right directly we were in the approach road.
We passed the lodges and were in our own
domain. Inveroran has a huge park: a belt

of forest trees runs all round, just inside the
wall, and then comes open moorland country
—mostly heather and silver birch thickets.
The deer were moving about in the distant
hollows; high up in the cloudless sky some
big hawk was soaring like an aeroplane. It
all seemed very primeval and stable; Europe
very far away.

Sandars and his satellites awaited us on the
perron. The chief got out after me, and handed
down the ladies. Miss Bacchus bundled up
the steps, but he led Helena by the hand. At
the door he let her go, stood, looked at her,
and then held out his arms. She faltered, then
stumbling forward, fell into them, broke into
sobs, and then fairly into a passion of crying.
He soothed her as if she had been a child, and
led her away. It was a most touching thing.
The fine generous old chap! My eyes were wet
over that. I wished Hector had been there.
Wynyard saw it, and turned away. Pierpoint
had gone in before it happened. I saw that
he and Wynyard exchanged no greeting, but
don't think that anyone else noticed it.

XIV

DAUGHTER OF THE HOUSE

WITHIN a week, if you'll believe me, she might have been there from the cradle. That shows you that she had a genius for being snug. I had been sure of it. Within ten days she ran the whole house. You caught yourself saying, I wonder how the deuce they got on before she was here! In that bachelor house, I can tell you, the difference was extraordinary— extraordinarily pleasant too. We all revelled in her.

That is our excuse for being engaged, as I know we were, in a highly immoral conspiracy to make a thing which was not all right seem as if it was. We were harbouring a runaway wife and trying to ignore the fact that she was a married woman. She was "daughter of the house," if you please, in defiance of Euphemia Grant, and the curse of the Mallesons. We were engaged in buoying up a bladder of fiction, which might break into thin air at any moment, or by any exaggerated breath. But

we were all at it, led by Wynyard, who had
been so put off by it at first. Wynyard swiftly
and finally fell in love with Helena. He
betrayed himself at every point, after his
own fashion. He became her shadow, and
said less than ever. It seems a stupid way
of making love, but she couldn't have enough
love, you see, and she read the nature of the
man. Pat followed, when he came home.
Thus she had the lot; and the chief was the
worst of them.

Not that the chief made love to her, of
course. He did what was far more effective
when he let her understand from the first that
his welfare and moral standing in his kingdom
were involved in her. Every act, every look,
every word (and with him word stood for
thought) implied it. It was a subtle form of
enchainment, for while she was absolute
mistress of her own head, heart, and will, he
let her see beyond dispute that, so far as his
were concerned, he had handed them up to
her discretion. And she wasn't the woman
to ignore responsibility. She felt it intensely.
It chastened and sobered her at every turn.
I was amused to watch her playing step-

mother to all these young men who adored her. Nothing could have been more effective. Pierpoint was as harmless as a sucking dove.

It wasn't our fault. We couldn't help it. Not only was she so pretty and so sweet; but she made us all so cozy. It began, I remember, by her taking over the flowers for the house. Sandars had always done them himself. She made a different thing of it. One became aware of flowers, and of her at the same time. The scents mingled, the associations interacted. As Pat said, you found out what "ripping things" flowers were, and how "ripping" she was, "in one act." She used to be down long before anybody else; and there was always something exciting for the breakfast table—and, always, a rose for the chief, in a vase by his plate. So it went on; one thing led to another. It was Miss Bacchus who put her in touch with Mrs. MacIntyre, the housekeeper, and with Rose, the cook. Then we found out that Helena herself was a good cook. Then that department fell to her. So it went on.

And they all liked her, and all accepted her upon the fictitious value. She was not Miss

Malleson, she was "the Baroness," but she
was taken as the lady of the house. She
wasn't treated as a visitor. There was no
question of a visit. Everything suggested
permanency. They asked her if the curtains
in her room would do "till next year." I
believe Sandars thought she had been born
there, had married, gone away, lost her husband and come back again. It is a fact that
Wilson, the head gardener, said, "Don't your
ladyship remember? We planted him on
Mafeking Day?" She had blushed and
laughed as she said, "Indeed, Wilson, I don't,"
but she was enormously pleased, and Sir
Roderick, I feel sure, would have liked to
raise his wages. It was awfully foolish,
awfully fond—but Lord! how happy they
were! Those three, the chief, Hector, Helena
herself—I believe that summer was for each
of them a time of golden haze, never hoped for,
never to be forgotten. I won't answer for the
others. Wynyard brooded upon his affair,
and while professing secrecy, at any rate to
himself, was transparently concerned with
Helena. Pierpoint sulked, and appeared to
shrink while you looked at him. That was

obviously because Wynyard was there. But he stuck it out, though Helena had very little to say to him, and didn't seem to have him at all at heart. It was curious how he had completely lost his conquering air. He was like a spent salmon.

An odd thing occurred. We thought it odd at the time. Helena had brought no maid with her, and there was a lot of talk about getting one for her. We were having tea. Pat slapped his leg and jumped up—"I've got it. Promote Ethel. She's always been a trump. She's just the sort." Pierpoint was handing tea-cake or muffins. He looked very black. "Rot!" he said. "Wouldn't do at all." He was as red as a peony, and hated it. Helena looked from one to another as if she wondered (a) why Pat had proposed the girl, (b) why Pierpoint' objected. The chief, who was rather slow at catching what we talked about, said, "Of course. Of course. Universally respected. Nobody could do so well," and promised that Helena should see her.

Pierpoint, however, was very much put out. He sulked for the rest of the day. I had my

own idea about it—which simply was that
he had tried at one time or another to make a
fool of the girl, and didn't care to have two
of his failures brought together. I think Miss
Bacchus had ideas too—but I kept away from
her. It was settled, however, by Ethel's
definitely refusing. She was perfectly respectful, I heard, but perfectly definite. She
couldn't, and she wouldn't. Sir Roderick was
very much offended, and, I believe, talked to,
her of "loyalty." She wouldn't do it, though.
Pierpoint recovered; but shortly afterwards
he went away—yachting, I understood, in
Norway. He seemed to me to have put
Helena out of his head; or he might have
been waiting for Wynyard to move.

Helena, naturally, was changed from what
she had been when I knew her before. From
being a reticent woman she was become transparently candid. You must be very comfortably off when you can afford to discuss
your own little weaknesses. She said to me
apropos of Ethel's refusal of the coveted office,
"Ethel is a beautiful girl, but she doesn't
like me. Do you think she knows about
me?"

I was embarrassed. This wasn't keeping up the conspiracy. I said, "She evidently doesn't know what everybody else knows about you."

"Ah," she said, "you are all too kind. You spoil me. But I love it—oh, I love to be spoiled!" Then her eyes shone very bright. "Now you will see. I will make Ethel like me."

I said, Was that worth while? And she looked at me, pondering—as if the question rather was, Was *I* worth while? She decided, apparently, that I was, for she took an air of decision. "Yes," she said, "it is necessary. I am greedy. I have a sweet tooth, as you say—and we say it too. I have a sweet tooth. I didn't know it—but it is true."

I said, "Oh, you'll get her—never a doubt of it. She's a nice, good girl, absolutely straight. I have known her for years. We are quite good friends. I dance with her once a year."

She opened her eyes. "You dance with Ethel?"

I explained about the servants' ball. "We all dance with her—if she'll have us. But she is in great demand. She's what we call 'the thing.' What Pat calls 'it.' "

She smiled, rather wisely, from under contracted brows. "Does Pierpoint call her 'it'?"

I did the best I could. "I don't suppose he does now, because obviously she is not 'it.' But I expect he did, in his day. Everybody did, until you taught them better. I assure you, she's a very nice girl indeed."

Helena threw up her brows, as if to shake Pierpoint off into the air, then nodded her head two or three times. "Yes, I like her. I will make her like me. You will see—you will see."

She began to talk about Hermione, her child—quite naturally, not concealing anything. She said that a very dear friend of hers—a Pole like herself—with whom she had exchanged a weekly letter for more than fifteen years, went to see Hermione once a week at the Convent where she was bestowed, and kept her regularly informed. She said:

"I suppose I ought not to do it, but I write to Hermione under cover to my friend, and she writes to me. My friend is Countess

Voss. If there were any trouble Hermione would go directly to her."

I said that must comfort her.

"Yes," she said, "it is comfortable. It is better than I could expect. She is happy with the nuns. They will not tease her. They know I should not allow it. They are very sensible ladies."

I ventured to ask how old Hermione was. "She is now twelve years," she said. "I have three years—a long time for me."

"To——?" I asked for form's sake.

"Before she leaves the nuns. After that it will be difficult. I don't know what I shall do, but I need not think of that yet."

"No, you have time enough for that," I said. "Meantime, you need not fret. You know that she loves you."

"Yes, indeed. She loves me." She said that softly, looking down at her hands. Then she added, still more softly, with a pretty sort of cooing, soothing note, "it is the dearest wish of my heart to have her here, with me, with all of you here. Then I shall have my heart quite full. There will be no room left in it."

I said, "Except for Ethel Cook."

She looked up shy, half-laughingly, "Oh, I'm not afraid of Ethel," she said.

That's what I call settling down, you know.

A visit which had been absurdly dreaded, passed off without trouble. Why should there have been trouble? Even if the Marchioness had caught at shreds of rumour, what did it all come to but that Pierpoint had flirted with a married woman? That's how we put it to each other in those days of happy pretence. All the same, the Marchioness came alone—without her girls. Her recognition of Helena was of a glittering kind, of the kind which takes nothing for granted. Not at all empressée, implying the possibility of something disagreeable on the sky-line. Wynyard said that she took Helena as one takes a snow shower on the hills. She didn't ask after the Baron, or make any personal references. She talked mostly about the Red Cross, I remember, and St. John of Jerusalem, whoever he might be. Helena talked about Greece and mentioned her dusky Princess Glinka with affectionate mockery. She even dragged

Hector in to confirm an anecdote, and once
spoke of Pierpoint by name. The Marchioness
smiled more glitteringly than ever, said it
must have been delightful, and slid off on to
some other subject. It was unfortunate, I
thought, that no other women were there.
Miss Bacchus had gone to drink tea in the
town. Mrs. Jack was golfing with Pierpoint.
She saw three men, and Helena. It was
impossible to prevent the impression of a snug
domestic interior, with a tutelary goddess.
The fact was that she had a very tutored
air upon her, soft, sweet and sedate. She was
almost sleek. She sat by the fire like a weel-
tappit hen, indeed, as if she had been born
to it. She couldn't help it. That was how
she felt about it. She had succumbed to the
prevailing fiction.

XV

INTERRUPTION

On August 13 I was again at Inveroran, but
for a very short visit. I had left London on
the night of the 11th, arrived on the afternoon
of the 12th, and was down early next morning,
hoping to shoot with the party, which was
small this year.

It was a day of dry heat. There was a faint
blue mist rapidly clearing before the sun.
The country all about was faintly bleached
with drought. The promise of the moment
was for torrid weather. It was not yet nine
o'clock, but the sky was white. The sea lay
like a sheet of burnished steel—motionless,
colourless.

Standing on the terrace, looking out over
the bay, I became gradually conscious of a
strange vessel anchored some half a mile out.
You know the way moored ships have of
seeming part of the landscape. I had to look
long before I made sure that she was new.
This was a large steam yacht—with two masts.

She was a white boat, with sharp bows,
apparently about eighty tons. The burgee
and the flag at the stern drooped like weed in
a windless air. I could swear that she hadn't
been there yesterday when my steamer brought
me up from Glasgow.

I stepped back into the breakfast-room and
asked Sandars about her. He had seen her.
She had been there at seven o'clock when he
got up. Mr. Fairfax, the factor, had been in;
he had asked him. But nobody seemed to
know. Sandars said a good many yachts
came in during the summer. The anchorage
was so good, he said. They didn't stay long.
They usually landed a large party for the
Abbey ruins (these are at Oranmouth and
considered very fine), and took luncheon. In
the afternoon they were away, said Sandars.

I went out again to have a look at her.
Black smoke straggled out of her funnel and
hung like a cloud above her. A motor launch
came round her stern and speeded for the
quay—two or three persons sat in it, one
stood up with glasses to his eyes. I ran back
into the house for some glasses, in my turn,
but by the time I had brought them to bear

the launch was under the land. I examined
the yacht carefully—there was nothing to be
seen. I saw a man in white jacket, apron and
cap pass along the deck. A cook, I judged.
There were no other signs of life. A few
shore boats hung about; but there was nothing doing.

People strayed in to breakfast. Hector
came up from the gardens. He was the first.
I showed him the yacht. To oblige me, he
looked at her; but his head was full of something or other, and he took no interest.
"Trippers," he said, with the glasses to his
eyes, and "Trippers," as he handed them
back to me. Then Pat came out, kilted and
brogued for the shoot, with shining morning
face and that air of perfect fitness for any
mortal thing which is so refreshing to jaded
Londoners. He was more alive to the picturesque. "Hulloa! A sail, a sail! What
have we here?" He looked long and earnestly.
"I bet you she's Italian," he said. "I bet
you," said I, for friendliness.

Then came Helena, all in cool white, and
kissed her two brothers, and shook hands with
me. "I'm going to get the chief's rose, if I

can find one," she said. "Who's coming?"

"I am." That was Pat. Hector had ranked himself without speech. "But I say," he went on, "do look at the strange craft. We are betting on her nation. I say, Italian. You have all Europe to choose from—but you can't have Italy, because that's bagged. Well, what do you say?"

Helena was looking. "She's very, very beautiful. White and gold—yes, I see the gold lines. And I see somebody aboard. In a chair. With coffee. With Turkish coffee. And cold water."

"Who is it? Masculine or feminine?—Say neuter, do. No, don't, because it might be improper." Pat looked carefully round, in case he had said what he ought not to have said.

But Helena took no notice of him. She was still looking. "I don't want to look any more," she said, and handed me the glasses. "I am going for the rose. The flag is Austrian." Her eyes loomed, big and heavy. She went away slowly, and Hector followed her without a word. She didn't lift her head so long as they were in sight.

I handed the glasses to Pat. I had seen the Austrian chequer-board flag stream out in the little local wind. Pat put down the glasses and looked at me. He was serious now.

"Austrian!" he said; and I echoed him, "Austrian!"

He said next, "Did you see that chap in the chair?"

"Yes," I said.

"There were two sticks on the deck. One on each side of him."

"I know," I said.

"Look here. What are we to do?"

I said, "What can we do? There's nothing to do. The less you do the better."

He took a turn and came back. "Do you think that *she* saw him?"

I said, "Yes, I do."

She didn't come to breakfast; but Hector saw it through. Directly it was over, he took Miss Bacchus apart and explained to her what had upset Helena. Miss Bacchus, like the Trojan she was, cried briskly, "Ho, that's the game, is it? Well, I'll go and talk

to her about it"—and went. The chief had
gone off with his letters and the paper to his
own room. Pat went out on a bicycle to
find out what was going on. Hector and I
beckoned Pierpoint to follow us. Wynyard,
who was finishing his breakfast, called out
that we should wait for him. He came after
us, his dog at his heels.

We went down to the river and sat there in
the arbour by the aviary. All the time we
were talking, little yellow and silvery birds
darted across and across like streaks of light.

Hector began on an uncertain note. "Pat's
gone down to the harbour to find out," he
said; "so perhaps we had better wait till we
hear what he says. What do you think?"
He addressed that question to me.

I said, "It doesn't much matter what Pat
says. You may take it as a certainty. I saw
him."

Wynyard was looking bleakly at Pierpoint,
who had his elbows on his knees and was
chewing a leaf. I hadn't reckoned on what
followed, I must say.

"You there," said Wynyard, with a kind of
croak in his voice, "you've brought this on us."

14

Pierpoint looked up, red all over, "I won't take this from you," he said. "You had better understand that."

But Wynyard didn't flinch. "Your d——d philandering has done it. Do you suppose you are the God of Love? Do you suppose von Broderode doesn't put it all down to your account? You fool. And do you suppose the Marchioness didn't tell him that Helena was here—and that you were here? Don't you think she owes you one for making a fool of that poor girl of hers? How many more women do you want about you?"

Wynyard was showing his teeth, and Pierpoint jumped up and towards him. I pulled him back; and then Hector had a chance of cutting in.

"You're only making mischief," he said to Wynyard. Surely you don't want to do that. And you seem to be reflecting on Helena, which I for one won't have. We came here to see what we could do for her—at least, I suppose we did." Pierpoint had walked away along the river.

Hector said, "Some one must go and tell my father. I think he'll be offended when he, finds out that we've discussed it without him."

Wynyard said, "I'll answer for *him*. But I tell you fairly, I won't answer for that chap." He jerked his head towards his retreating brother. "He's rotten," he added.

We let that go by and listened to Hector. He said that he wished to face the Baron at once. He proposed to go and see him in the course of the morning; but when I asked him what he thought of saying to him, he wasn't very definite. Discuss the situation! Wynyard scoffed at that—but Hector insisted that he was right. He said that the man must have come here with something in his mind. Well, he hoped to find out what that was. Meantime he hoped that Helena would keep to the grounds. We wrangled about this for sometime without getting at close quarters. Hector then said he must go and see his father—and just at that moment Pat came on the scene.

He was out of breath and excited. "I say, I've found out all about it. I saw the harbour-master. She's the *Coryphæus* of Trieste— belongs to a Count Jellyfish or something.

Wait, I'll tell you." He produced a paper and read from it—"'S.Y. *Coryphœus*, port of origin, Trieste. . . owner, Count Szombar Jelacics'—did you ever hear such a name? Then I went up to the Marine, where they are all staying. I saw Jellykicks in the hall. He's got bunches of hair in his ears—and the rest of it cut *en brosse*. He *is* a hairy man. Tall chap—wears stays. Then there's another man—sandy man with a perfectly round face—all red. And on the terrace I saw old Welcome Highlander and a cigar. So there you are."

I said, "If you take my advice, you fellows, you will leave them entirely alone. You will do literally nothing, and you will go on as if literally nothing had happened. If you make the first move you will put yourselves in the wrong. I suppose it may be said that you *have* made it already, and *have* put yourselves in the wrong, but we'll leave it at that. He's here to bore her into going back. He has come out here, in my belief, to put you in a false position. Well, you'll get there if you do anything. Legal process is really his only remedy—and that's very little. If he won't take it, don't try to force him."

I didn't convince Hector, I could see. Pat
was a boy, and of course wanted to have a
slap at them. I didn't expect to convince
him. But Wynyard took my side.

"I think he's right. I think we must sit
it out." Pat said—to my surprise—"Can't
she be got out of it?"

Wynyard said, No, she couldn't. He said,
if she went away, she'd be hunted. Once
start her on a run and there'd be no stopping
it. She couldn't be better off than she was
here. It was up to us to see that, whoever
suffered by it, it wasn't she.

And then into the midst of us she came, and
stood looking from one to the other of four
men who loved her. She was pale, and her
eyes were heavy.

We all stood up and waited for her. It
was no time for forms and ceremonies. Not
one of us disguised our feelings.

Pat broke the silence. "Where's Pierpoint?"

She said, "He is with his father."

"Does father know?" That was Pat again.

"Yes," she said. "I told him. He wishes
to see you all in his room. But I came because

I thought that I must see you first." Then
she hesitated, and I saw her eyes fill to the
brim. She held out her arms—"Let me go,"
she said. "Let me go."

Wynyard threw up his hand. He was
crimson. "I'll die before you shall go," he
said. His eyes were burning and seemed to
smite her. She couldn't meet them; she
quailed.

Hector said—and he was at the opposite
pole from his hot and furious brother—"At
whatever cost, you must do as you wish. If
you want to leave us, it must be so. If one
thing is certain, it is that you are free."

Poor dear! If one thing was certain it was
that she was not free. But one couldn't say
a word.

She went on talking, as if to herself, as if
protesting to herself. There were tears in her
eyes, tears in her voice. "I have been happy
—you were all so kind—how could I be anything but happy? But it is my business to
be unhappy. I must not stop to think about
it." She shook her head, and wiped her tears
away. "Oh, why did you make me happy?"
she said to Hector, with a gentle reproach.

"Why did you do it?" It was absurd, but
very touching. Why on earth? Just for an
idea!

Hector would have spoken, but Wynyard
brushed him and his words away. "My
dear," he said, "you are going to be happy.
That's why you are here—and that's why we
are here. Come now and talk to the chief.
We'll see you through."

He turned her; he turned Hector. She
went up the slope between them, her head
hanging. Pat and I followed.

In the chief's room, backed by the antlered
heads, and long narrow portraits of bewigged
Jacobites, we found ourselves in a council of
war. Sir Roderick sat, Pierpoint stood beside
him. I thought he had taken that place for
shelter—but it looked bad. It was his presence, of course, that put us in the wrong. We
crowded to the door at first. Helena crossed
the room and went straight to the old man.
He put his arm around her and kissed her
forehead. Then he told her that she couldn't
stop here while we talked. He asked her to
trust him to do what was best for her and for

the family, and said that he would come and
see her directly he had talked to us. She went
away quite quietly, without raising her head.

We talked, as usual, all at sixes and sevens.
We were in a tight place undoubtedly, because we wanted two incompatible things.
We wanted Helena to be happy, and we
wanted to have it out with the Baron. Now
she couldn't be happy if she stayed with us,
nor if she left us and went back to her husband.
And we couldn't have it out with von Broderode either, because we couldn't drag her
name into our debates with him. Only two of
us, myself and Wynyard, had an idea of what
the Baron really meant to do. The chief
thought that he meant to carry her off; and
I believe that Hector suspected it. What
Pierpoint thought I couldn't make out. Not
that it mattered. He had gone to pieces.
We were to know why that was, in time; but
we none of us knew it then. Miserable wretch
that he was! He saw that we all despised
him—and yet, it's all very well, but what he
could have done, I really don't know. He
should never have come to Inveroran, you
say? Of course he should not. But he was

one of those men who only seriously begin to
want a thing when it is beyond dispute that
they haven't a ghost of a chance of getting it.
I am sure that he began really to desire Helena
after his check at Wynyard's hands. I think
also that her indifference to him was a per-
petual sting to him. At this moment I believe
that he was sincerely in love with her. But
nothing is more certain than that she neither
knew nor cared whether he was or not. She
was over head and ears in love with Inveroran,
and herself a daughter of the house. She may
have loved him once; and he had failed her.
Yet here she was! Here she was in this
house, with every male inhabitant of it, you
may say, at her feet. And if she liked the
feeling of that, it's no wonder. There were
better men than Pierpoint there. Hector was
a better man, Wynyard was a better man.
Either Hector or Wynyard would have thrown
up his inheritance for her. Hector would
have taken her to Paris or London and taught
her the uses of love in a life of obscure work.
I can see Hector, in a Chelsea studio or Soho
attic, as happy as only an artist can be. He
would have been a poet, of course, and I don't

doubt a pretty bad poet; but he would have
been happy, and she would have adored him
and thought him a prince of poets. Wynyard
would have gone to Canada with her, or to an
Argentine ranch. He would have given her
half a dozen children, and she would have
thought him a king of cowboys. She was
like that. She had a sweet tooth, as she said.
She wanted to be loved, but much more than
that, she wanted to love.

Now Pierpoint, once, had very nearly swept
her off her feet. It was he who had persuaded
her to run. He had carried her passions,
inflamed her imagination; but no more. He
had stopped. He had *been* stopped, but she
didn't know it. Pierpoint had wanted her,
but had never loved her as either of the others
would. Pierpoint was a voluptuary, a pre-
cocious Don Juan. Helena was no fool. She
had her feelings like other people and they
had swamped her judgment. But when the
floods subsided, the wits returned to her. He
had pushed her over the edge, and hadn't
followed her. Well, she had learned to do
without him. If she had been let alone she
would have done very well without matri-

mony at all. She had plenty of love on hand
without that.

But here, up against us, was that brisk-
minded Baron von Broderode with but one
idea before him, and no scruples about happiness or unhappiness. What were we to do
against him?

While the chief listened to us, I could see
which way he himself inclined. He loved this
daughter of the house so much that he would
have sunk his chieftainship for her, I felt sure.
But what he loved still more was his own
dignity. He had stiffened himself into intend-
ing to keep her and the chieftainship, too.
His difficulty was a not unnatural one. He
was casting about for a moral gloss to overlay
his resolution. He was sharp enough to see
the rent in Hector's armour. The poor
Hector kept saying that Helena must be made
happy. Ridiculous—it was only too clear
that whatever happened Helena must be
unhappy. And, although he admired it he
couldn't quite bring himself round to Wynyard's frank declaration of piracy. "She's
here, and she shall stay here," said Wynyard
over and over again. This was accompanied

by young Patrick's "Good man —good old
Wynyard!" By degrees and degrees he slid
gently down into the fine old position of the
man of property—the man in possession.
"No, no, sir, possession is nine points of the
law. We can't have that interfered with"
—and "What, sir! A man comes and flouts
me on my own land! He brings his ship into
my waters, and stays at my own hotel—and
—and threatens me, by Gad! No, no—we
can't have that, my lads." So he comforted
himself. It didn't matter; it was established
that Helena was not to go.

Nothing was to be done for the present.
We were to carry on as usual. We would
shoot, we would fish, play golf; we would
show ourselves abroad. All was to be according to the time-honoured ways of the Malleson
clan. "They will stand by us—I know them—
bless their red hearts!" said the old chief.
But Wynyard didn't echo him. Wynyard
didn't care whether they stood by him or not.

At the close of our meeting Sir Roderick
went off to see Helena. I'm told the meeting
was very affecting. She cried in his arms, as
she had done when she first came, and he

soothed her with his loving and very possibly
foolish old words.   Then Pierpoint came in
—looking, Miss Bacchus said, as if he was
going to the dentist—and (as even she allowed)
behaved well.   He asked her to forgive him;
he asked her to forget him.   Fatuous young
man! She had done that long ago. Of course
he really meant, *not* to forget him.   But he
might have spared his breath.   He was
nothing to her.   But she gave him a sad and
gracious smile—and I suppose he built upon
it, for he began to lay siege to her again
from that hour.

Sir Roderick, however, was paramount.
She couldn't stand up against him.   After all
she may have reasoned, it was her own doing.
She had sent a letter to his bosom, and followed it there in person.   If he had accepted
her it wasn't for her to deny him.   He was
going to be besieged in his own house—and
here he was patting her shoulder and taking it
as all in the day's work.   She could only listen
to him and be grateful.   All should come right.
Would she not trust them, since they were one
and all for her?   What could she say?   She
gave herself to his arms, and he led her away.

XVI

THE SIEGE OPENS

AFTER luncheon we all felt adventurous. Pat
and I said that we would go down to the shore
and look about us. Hector and Wynyard took
Helena up into the hills. Pierpoint said that
he should go and give Mrs. Jack a round on
the links, and would drive her down in his cart.

Pat was in high fettle. It was all pure joy
to the likes of him. I believe that he had a
revolver on his person somewhere. I recognized his sword-stick. Then there was his
huntsman's knife. He was armed to the
teeth. We took a short cut over the foothills which they call the braes, and by a lane
which brings you out by the Western Bank
about midway of the main street. A little
below this junction of roads is Rosemount.
I noticed at once that there was something
going on here. The blinds were up, the
windows open. A man was scraping the front
door preparatory to a new coat of paint. All
agog as we were for the unexpected, here
was a flick on the cheek.

222

We walked up the short circular sweep, and Pat accosted the painter with a "Good day, Donald."

"Good day, Mr. Patrick. A fine afternoon we are having."

"First-rate," says Pat. "I say, what are you up to? Have you got a tenant for this place?"

The man busied himself over his job. "I couldn't say," we heard, and then—"But I believe." That's as near as a Highlandman will go. Pat took it as it was meant.

"Oh, you have? I wonder who that will be?"

No answer to that. We walked past him into the empty house. The passage ran straight through past the staircase, down a step, and out, past the kitchen and scullery to a glass door. Beyond that we saw a decent garden, with a large sycamore tree on a square of grass. Then came a privet hedge— kitchen-garden beyond. The two front rooms had bow windows and a full view of Main Street either way. They were well above the containing wall of the front garden.

"A fine strategic point," I said; and then Pat jumped to my suspicion.

"I say, do you suppose he's going to *live* here?"

I said, "That's my little idea."

He looked at me with concern.

"She'll hate that."

"She mustn't know it," I said.

Pat tossed his head. "Know it! That's absurd. She's bound to know it. She knows everything—God knows how." Then he wondered, and admired. "By George, if you're right—and I believe you are—he's a bit of a great man, is the Baron. He don't do things by halves."

"He's a German," I said. "They don't."

"I thought Austrians were slackers?" he said.

I told him that Austrians were Germans with a high glaze. "But we've scratched the glaze for this one," I said, "and are up against the German."

We were in one of the bow-windows, looking out—which was foolish of us. Just then two strangers turned in at gate.

"Trapped!" said Pat to me. "What shall we do now?"

"Stop where we are," I told him. "That's all we can do."

The two men were dressed with extreme elegance—dark-blue pea-jackets, white ducks, white shoes, white yachting-caps. One was tall and slim. As Pat had reported, he was very hairy. From one point of view he was like a walking whisker. He had cavernous eyes, which at close quarters were of fathom-less dark. The other had a more Saxon, appearance. He was very fair, very pink, very round-faced. He wore an eyeglass.

They saw us, straightened their backs, and quickened their pace. They entered the house and stood behind us in the doorway. I turned, Pat turned; we took off our hats and made to retire, doing our best to assume that nothing had happened.

Neither of them returned the salute. The tall and hairy gentleman said nothing. The shorter man, with a great deal of colouring in his round face, spoke with excitement surging in his voice, and giving it a bell-like resonance.

"That," he said, "was private property. It was a private house."

I said, "I'm very sorry. It was inexcus-able."

15

He patted the ground with his toe. "It was quite so," he said.

The other man looked at the ceiling and murmured to it, "Impossible," in French.

"You must let me explain," I said. "I did not understand that the house was taken. I thought it was to let."

"Not at all, not at all," said the Saxon. "It was to let—yes. But now it is not any longer to let."

"*Impossible!*" murmured his friend, still to the ceiling, "*impossible!*"

"In that case," I said, "I have the honour to leave you in possession, with many apologies."

They made elaborate room for us. They took off their caps and almost swept the floor with them. We retired, feeling what we deserved to feel.

But our adventures were not over. Rounding the gate, we came plump upon the Baron in a bath-chair, which a seaman from the yacht was pushing. By the side of him was the dark-skinned woman whom I had heard called Teresa Visconti.

We were so much taken aback that Pat

lost his head and I the use of my limbs. I
mean that Pat, abruptly enough, jerked out,
"Hullo, Baron," in his freshest and youngest
voice, and that I held out my hand to him.

He was severely changed in looks, poor chap,
but very gay. Disease had deepened the lines,
and Nature surged outwards where she could.
His eyes were heavily bagged, his cheeks had
hollowed; he seemed to hold his head sideways in order to look up at us. His gnarled
hands clasped on his stick shook fearfully.
But he was his old galliard self within walls.

"Ha!" he said, "here's my old-young
friend, the cool cucumber. How are you?
And how is your friend Patrick? Quite well?
That is excellent. With me it is only so-so.
But you see I remember Inveroran. I like it
so much that after two years I remember it,
and the Games of Odysseus. And the ball—
what? You have a ball this year at the
Castle?"

I said that old customs die hard at Inveroran. Whereupon he bent his shaggy brows
upon me, and said in his throat, "Yes, they
die hard."

Then he changed the subject and asked us,

How did we like his house? Pat said it was a good house. He addressed the next remark to me:

"I owe you that house of mine—do you remember? We talked of Peter Grant, and you told me of the lady, the *bonne amie*, his ancestress? Well, Mr. Peter Grant sells to me. That is now my castle at Inveroran. The Englishman's house is so-called, eh? It is a fine prospect. Don't you agree with me?"

I agreed that it would suit his purpose excellently. He said, "My purpose! What do you know of my purpose, ha?"

One of the Baron's most valid qualities was that he very rarely got angry. I thought that he was going to break out now—but he caught himself in the act, and bent off on a side track. He turned, beaming, on Pat. "And what will Mr. Patrick be doing in these piping times?" he asked. "How goes it with Oxford nowadays?"

Patrick grinned and said that Oxford was going strong when he last saw it. They exchanged a few pleasantries before we left him. He waved his hand to us and was wheeled up the sweep of his outpost.

We walked down the Main Street, and I had just said that we had learned one thing at least, which was that the Baron expected a long leaguer, when Pat became confidential. He took my arm.

"I say," he said, "he's rather an old sportsman, isn't he?"

I said, Certainly he was.

Pat added more of his inverted praise—such as that he seemed not half a bad old chap—and then went on to muse.

"I suppose she can't stand him—at any price? I don't know, you know, but I should have said he could be good company."

I didn't feel that I could discuss such delicate matters as underlay these youthful misgivings. What I did say was that Helena had seemed very depressed when she was with him, and was only depressed now when she heard that he was near her again. That didn't look well, I said. I admitted that it couldn't be used as an argument, but reminded him that, for what it was worth, she had been extraordinarily happy with us.

He was full of thought. He said, "I know, I know," And then jumped into altruism.

"Of course the decent thing to do would be for him to say, Look here, I can see you are as happy as a bird up there. All right—I'm glad—God bless you. And then clear out! Mind you, that's what old Hector would do —to-morrow. But the Baron don't look at it like that."

"Not at all," I said. "The Baron says, She belongs to me. I bought and paid for her. And she's useful—she amuses me."

Pat said, "Oh, shut up. I don't believe it. I've half a mind to go back and ask him."

"For heaven's sake, don't," I said. "He'd make things worse than they are."

"Well," Pat said, "if you ask me, I don't think they could be much worse. Are you going to tell them what's happened?"

I said that I should tell Hector, but nobody else. He said, "Poor old Hector. He's badly knocked over this. So's Wynyard."

I said, "I must say that if she had to run away, I wish it had been Hector or Wynyard who had persuaded her. There wouldn't have been this absurd siege—and—oh, well, it's no good talking about that."

Pat said, "I know what you were going to

say. Pierpoint's a rotter—but there he is. And she don't care two straws for him. And, after all, he didn't run away with her."

"Why the deuce can't Pierpoint go abroad?" I snapped out. "The Baron might follow him to Canada."

Then Pat looked at me. "You don't think the Baron cares about Pierpoint! I'll bet you what you like he's never given him a thought."

There it was. Of course he hadn't.

"Hector," Pat said, "would never have run away with her. He'd have been in love with her, and she with him—and for that reason alone he wouldn't have done her any harm. He couldn't. He's got such a nice mind."

"I think you are right about Hector," I agreed. "He's not a strong man, but he's a gentleman. Now Wynyard——"

Again Pat looked at me. "Do you want my real opinion? I believe that Pierpoint would have got her if he could, but that Wynyard wouldn't let him."

Then in fair exchange I gave him my own real opinion, which was that Helena didn't want to run away with anybody in particular, but was perfectly happy as she was.

All she wanted was for everybody to be in love with her.

Pat shook his head knowingly. "Well, everybody is—including old Two-Sticks. In a way, you know. You are, I suppose——"

I owned to it, "in a way."

"Well, so am I—in a way."

"And what's your way?" I said.

He told me. "I want her to be happy—I want her to be about to look at—to be there when I come back, and to make things go. But I don't want to run away with her. That would spoil the fun. And besides—oh, well—it wouldn't do."

I adjured him to continue; and he made a rather acute remark. "She's one of those sort of women," he said, "who lend themselves to exclusiveness. If I were to let myself fall in love with her—in that sort of way, you know—I should want to lock her up in a castle and have her to myself."

"That's how the Baron feels about it," I said.

"Yes," said Pat, "I know he does. And we can't have that—can we?"

I said, We should have to see about it.

XVII

HECTOR IN FORCE

I HAD seen some curious looks bent upon us
during our afternoon in the town, and felt
pretty sure that the place was humming with
surmise. Mrs. Chevenix reported as much
when we met her before dinner. She said she
was bespattered with looks, and thought that
she didn't much care about it. "Really, I
think the poor dear will have to go," she said
"The whole town must know about it by this
time, and you know how they feel about such
things."

I said, No doubt. But would Sir Roderick
give her up? She didn't know him as well
as I did. Poor Helena was now not much
more than a symbol.

She said, Surely it could be arranged. Her
advice was that Hector and I should see the
Baron and try to make terms. I didn't tell
her then that I *had* seen him; but I did tell
her what I thought we were in for. I told her
about Rosemount and the Baron's two friends.

233

"We are besieged, you know. Inveroran is become a second Troy, and the ships of the Achaians are in the roadstead. Menelaus is putting up his hut."

She was amused. "And Achilles—is he there?"

"I've seen him to-day. He's a hairy man, but very elegant. However, he can't talk Trojan."

"And will they get in on a wooden horse?" she asked me.

I said, "They'll get in on a high horse, if we're not careful."

She looked at me, lowered her voice. "You really think they will——?"

I said, "I do think so. They'll turn the whole place against us, except for a few of the Clan Malleson. It's rank nonsense, you know, because you aren't bound to have a man to stay with you; but the trouble is with Pierpoint. If it's known—as of course it is—that he's thrown up his commission, they'll put two together—and make a couple. But I sharply suspect that we're in for a fight. Pierpoint won't go, and the chief won't let Helena go either. He has got his back up; but so has von Broderode. However, I'll tell Hector what you say. I'm quite willing to go down with him—if we are allowed."

She told me more. "Helena is a strange creature. She has a perfect hunger for people. Do you know that she has won over that good-looking maid who wouldn't have anything to do with her? She told me just before I came down that she was much happier now. I asked her, Why? 'Oh,' she said, 'because I have made great friends with Ethel.' Ethel! I didn't know who on earth she meant—but it's the maid. I asked her how she had done it. She said, 'Oh, I told her of my troubles, and we cried together. I feel better.' She told me that the girl had troubles too—and you know what that usually means."

I protested strongly. I said there wasn't a more virtuous young woman in England; but Mrs. Jack said that you never knew. However, Helena couldn't tell her any more because she didn't know any more. But wasn't Helena extraordinary? she said. "If your troubles were her troubles, I don't think

you'd talk about them to another man's
maids, do you?" I didn't think you would.

Mrs. Jack began again. "Oh, and there's
another thing that she said. I must tell
you. She said, 'I am sure that Ethel can
help me. You'll see that she will.' I asked
her how? She didn't know, but she was quite
sure."

There was no doubt that Helena was in
much better spirits. I observed her at dinner,
and again afterwards when we were in the
drawing-room, doing our respectable best to
pretend that nothing had happened. I saw
her the centre of a group by the fire—for the
nights were chill although we were in mid-
August, and the log fire made a *point d'appui.*
Pat was with her, talking nonsense while he
held out silk for her to wind; old Laura
Bacchus was near-by, twinkling while she took
it all in and absorbed it into her seasoned old
head. Wynyard stood with his back to the
mantelpiece, frowning down, but evidently
at peace with the world. Helena talked and
flashed her eyes, softly bright, now at Pat on
his knees before her, once or twice quickly up
at Wynyard. Sometimes she telegraphed over

to Mrs. Chevenix, who was playing piquet with the chief. Pierpoint sat by himself, reading. I wondered over the scene—and as I wondered, Hector, who was with me, drew me apart. We went out into the hall.

There he said, after some preface about his wonder whether he ought to tell me or not—which I solved for him by saying that I was only stopping here to be of use, and that if I couldn't know what was going on I could be of no use and had better clear—it was then that he said, "She has dismissed Pierpoint." That shook me to the core, as Pat says.

"What do you mean—?" Then he told me of the scene already related, where Pierpoint solemnly asked to be forgiven, and was forgiven. So Pierpoint, Hector thought, was out of it.

So did I think at the time. "No wonder she is happier. She has done the right thing."

"She has done the only thing," he said.

"Her next move will be to go back to her Baron, you'll see." But he said, No, to that.

He said, "She won't go back. She may want to run away—for our sakes. But she won't go back to him, because she's afraid to.

I think myself that she would like to go back to Vienna and into a convent. She could see the child then, and not be in any danger. She has got to hate von Broderode—to hate and to dread him."

I asked, "How do you know, Hector?"

"She told us so—Wynyard and me this afternoon. She talked with absolute freedom, as if we were her blood-brothers. She said that she had been wicked, but that it was over. She said that she didn't intend to be wicked any more. That was how she put it. And then she said quite calmly, 'I have been wicked, but I have learned by it. I have learned how to be good. I could not go back to *him* (she never names him, you know, or calls him her 'husband') now—for that would be shameful for me. I would stay with you all if I could be allowed. There would be no harm—except to you. That is why I hope you will let me go home."

"How did Wynyard take it?" I wanted to know.

He said, "She has a great power over Wynyard. She knew that she could do what she liked with me. All her coaxing and

confidence was directed to him. She took his
arm and reasoned with him. He didn't say
anything—either for or against; but I don't
think he will be much trouble."

Then I told him what Pat and myself had
let ourselves in for. He said at once, "If
she knows this it will settle it. She will go.
But if my father knows it he won't let her.
This will infuriate him. He'll connect it
with the Malleson Curse." He looked at me
with wide, serious eyes. "And, of course, it
does connect with it—remarkably. You see
that?"

I said that I saw what he meant. Provi-
dence did not intend there to be a daughter in
Inveroran. The Baron was the instrument of
Heaven. That was it!

He took it with the utmost seriousness.
"We are bound to fight it. And we will fight
it. I must tell my father of this."

He wouldn't hear of going to see the Baron.
He was deeply incensed by what I had told
him—so much so that he failed, I thought, to
appreciate the science and capacity for action
of the enemy. In fact, I had begun with a
nerveless idealist and had turned him into a

passion-swept clansman, all raw head and
bloody bones.

He left me and went over to his father. He
stood by him, watching the game for a little;
then I saw him put his hand on the chief's
shoulder. The old man finished out his hand,
and then bowed to his opponent and got up.
Hector told him. I saw the news catch him
about the midriff and flood upwards to his
face. His bald head was suffused with crimson. He looked like an affronted wild beast
—a stag or a bull startled in front of his
feeding herd. They made a fine pair, the
two of them; for Hector was flushed and
fierce.

The chief, amid the concern of all present,
signalled to Wynyard and Pierpoint to follow
him. They obeyed at once, without any fuss.
Pat jumped up to go with them. His father
frowned, faltered—then allowed it. They
took no notice of me, and I made no effort to
follow them out. Directly they were gone
Helena fled across the room to Miss Bacchus,
and knelt by her side. As for me, I was very
uncomfortable where I was, and not very
clear where else I could be. At any rate I

thought that I would leave the ladies alone. I took a cigarette in the hall and walked about on the terrace.

I may have been there the better part of an hour. It was a beautiful, soft, clear night. The stars were brilliant, but there was no moon. Peace was abroad; the river tinkled below me in the dark; the owls shrilled as they quested. Man, as usual, seemed jarringly out of place in such a world as this, because while he so plainly didn't belong to it, he was so plainly doing what the rest of it was after. Those owls were hunting mice; out in the thickets there were stoats after the blood of flying rabbits. Foxes were abroad quick-nosed for hens. Great trout in the pools were scattering shoals of fry. It was a world of warfare; and there were my friends of old, my hosts, at the same red game. Helena was the prize. Down in the town, men were laying schemes for her; up here too were men, who had her, devising how best to keep her. What did all this mean? Must we give up the game? Were we indeed stoats and foxes—wolves in coats and trousers? I was

16

in a cynical mood. Was not this what it came to?

Out of the dark came a white figure. It was Helena herself.

She passed quite close to where I was leaning over the balustrade. I had seen her face like a pale disk. But she did not come alone; she was accompanied by a woman in black, whose face also I saw like a grey moon beside hers. Helena was talking vehemently. "I must—I tell you I must—but not alone. I am afraid of him too much. But you will come with me—you are so strong. I know that you will. . . ." They passed on along the terrace and I heard no more. They did not return; they had gone down the steps, probably to the river walk. I had no doubt as to who her companion was. It was her new friend Ethel Cook. Extraordinary that she should have picked out that girl! She had dear old Laura Bacchus, and Mrs. Chevenix, a brick, if ever there was one—but she chose to confide in a maid! It was pure instinct, of course. Women jump at these things, or we think so. But they communicate with each other in ways that men will never understand. I wondered whether Ethel would go with her, whether they would cut the knot that way—and was still wondering when Hector came out and called me. I answered his whistle and he came down.

He apologized for leaving me in the lurch. It was become now, he said, so purely a personal matter that he had not dared to suggest my presence to his father, who would not have liked it. "He is so edgy just now," said Hector, "that he don't like Pat to be present, just because he had talked to von Broderode."

I laughed. "Poor old Pat! He did it in the simplest way. He's not such a Highlander as most of you. It's Oxford."

Hector said quietly, "I was at Cambridge, as you know. But I understand my father's feeling. But however—" he broke away. "We have had it out at last. We are going to see it through. There will be lots of trouble. The town will make difficulties, and so will the country. The clansmen up the glens will hold by us. We are going to carry on."

"As if nothing had happened?" I asked.

He said, "Precisely. We feel that this matter of the legend, curse, which you choose,

must be faced. There never has been a
daughter of this house—it does so happen.
Now there is one. If we give way, my father
feels that—I agree with him; we all do——"

"Well? Put it definitely, for my plain
intelligence," I said.

"I'll try," said Hector. "We all feel that
if we surrender Helena now, we shall be giving
in to tradition, with unfortunate results."

"Do you seriously think that the results, if
any, of your allowing her to go back could by
any possibility be worse than those of her
staying on here? I really want to understand," I explained.

Hector said, "Yes, we do. If she leaves us
we establish a record against ourselves. People
will believe in the curse. If she stays, the
man will get sick of it, and go. He must die
very soon. You tell me he is much worse.
When he is dead the matter can be regularized.
Then she will no doubt marry Pierpoint."

"I am certain that she won't," I told him.
"She will never have anything to do with
Pierpoint again. After all, my dear chap," I
said, "what *has* she had to do with him?
Aren't you lending yourself to silly scandal-

mongering among the townsfolk by continuing
the legend that she nearly ran away with
him? The facts are that Pierpoint wanted
her to, and that she didn't. There are no
other facts, so far as I know."

Hector looked very stiff and solemn. "We
can hardly discuss it," he said. "But seeing
what she said this afternoon I don't suppose
you'll dispute that she also thought of an
elopement. As for the townspeople—what
sticks in their gizzards is that Pierpoint is
here with her—and that the Baron is *there*
without her."

"All right," I snapped out, "then why the
devil don't Pierpoint go away?"

Hector looked pained. "*After* the Baron's
arrival? Do you think that would help us?"

Of course it wouldn't. So then I attacked
him on the other side of the matter. How did
he know that she didn't want to go?

He said that he didn't believe that. She
was too fond of his father, and too apt for
happiness here to give it up lightly. Besides
that, she was morbidly afraid of Broderode.
He was on her nerves.

I said, "Well—we won't argue about it.

We can't. But I seriously hope that you won't let there be any constraint put upon her. If you do that—if there is any sign of that—I must go. Indeed, I must go pretty soon, at all events. I am very little use to you here. Don't, however, force me to go. I'm entitled to say that."

He assured me earnestly that there would be no compulsion. He said, "She had put matters as right as they could be put, of her own accord. They could be no more right if she left us to-morrow. That being so, there was no reason in the world why she should distress herself."

We both looked round. She was returning with her maid, and this time she saw us. She didn't falter or turn aside, but she disengaged her arm, and while Ethel Cook went on, stayed to talk to us. "We have been down by the river. It is so still that you can hear the fishes' lips as they rise to the fly. And all so beautiful—so beautiful—that it made me cry. I would like to be as beautiful as a summer night."

Hector said, "You are more beautiful than that." She didn't rise to it.

"Ah, no, indeed. If I were you would all be happy in this lovely place—and there would be no terrible things between you. Oh, what can I do? You have been so kind to me, I feel that I must do something."

Hector said, "My dear, be kind to my father, who loves you very much, and has never had a daughter."

She covered her face with her hands; I felt that she was crying. We both stood still, not daring to attempt consolation.

She mastered her passion and uncovered her face, but she clasped her hands under her chin. "He knows that I love him. If he needs me I will stay with him. It is the least I can do. What do I matter? Is he there? I will go to him now." And she went lightly and fleetly away.

XVIII

THE BATTLE SWAYS

WE rode up Glen Oran to the Clan meeting at Broken Cross; but a good deal happened before that, enough to remind us that we were really besieged. The rumours flying about the town and countryside focussed at last upon a deputation. Before that there had been pulpiteering at work. I don't know that the Mallesons were prayed for by name, but that they were obliquely prayed for I do happen to know. Then there were two letters in the local paper, one signed *Ruat Cœlum* and another *Anxious Mother of Seven*, which were guardedly referred to in a leading article. The time was coming on for the Gathering, and something must be done.

So the deputation came, and I caught sight of them from the terrace. Three black-coated gentlemen, obviously clerical, and one tall and lean man in riding-breeches and a checked cap. The chief had been persuaded not to see them—it was put to him on the

248

score of his dignity; and it may even be that he guessed he would lose his temper. Anyhow he wasn't there, and Hector saw them alone for about half an hour. Everybody was very polite, he said, and no names were named. Refreshments were served, and they went away. He was reticent about it, and I didn't press him; but I collected that the Annual Sports Meeting would *not* be held in the Port Field as usual, because, as I understood, the Deputation had said that the Town would be unable to support it, in view of public opinion. Here was a definite Act of War, and the meeting of the Clan at Broken Cross was to answer it.

The summons was sent round by night— a picturesque ceremony. The messengers gathered in front of the Castle. They all had unlighted torches. Sir Roderick and his sons, Helena with the ladies staying in the house, and myself stood on the steps. The chief gave out the message in Gaelic, which was received with perfect silence. Then Hector produced a lighted torch of resinous pine and stood at the foot of the steps. The men came and lighted their brands from his

and the whole forecourt flared and gloomed
as the lights wavered in the night wind.

They turned to the terrace; they sped
down the slopes—it was a strange and
romantic sight. We saw them dive down the
steep banks of Oran and ford the water,
throwing up into full vision as they did so
the very fronds of the fern on the further
shore, the very stones and eddies of the swift
river. After that they separated, and we
could watch, as it were, meteor paths to all
quarters of the East, South and North, and
see them rise and pause, dip and pursue, wax
and wane, according as the boulder-strewn
tracks held them. Remote as I was by breed-
ing and temper from the Gael, one could not
but be struck by the intensity of their devotion
to an idea. Sir Roderick Malleson had little
to do with it; Pierpoint and his unlawful prac-
tice less. It was the Clan which these fleet
and intent messengers were serving, just as
certainly as the Jacobite rising of 1745 had
not been for the worthless rip Charles Edward
but for a much bigger thing.

The meeting was for that day week, and in
the interval little or nothing happened. The

house settled itself to a new condition of things, and outwardly with very little difference. The young men shot and fished; the women talked and worked, if they did not accompany the men. Pierpoint seemed to be taking his rebuff quietly. It had sobered him down. There was nothing of Lovelace or Don Juan Osorio about him now. He took his part quietly, but efficiently, in the sporting exercise which seemed to be our be-all there.

Helena and the old chief became inseparable. She rarely left him for long, and I think never unless she knew what he was doing or how he was provided for. I had an idea that he was her only justification for staying where she was. I thought that, like nearly all of us, she had juggled with her conscience, to keep it quiet. It was as if she said, "I am naturally a pious and good woman, who yielding to a sudden fire of the mind have fallen into wrong-doing. I have put away the wrong from me, and out of it there has grown an innocent and honest use to which I can devote what is still innocent and honest in me. That is what I am doing now. Consider that, Conscience, and let me alone."

But if the chief was her strength, the Lord knows she was his. He overflowed with affection for her. She was the darling of his heart, the joy and pride of his eyes. I think it would have gone hard with him if she had left him just then. He was by no means a wise man; he was, in fact, a perfect child in his passionate impulses and inconsiderate acts. But he had a great heart—and enshrined her in the midst of it, and turned all the fire and flood of it to her honour. An odd result of this was that she became unapproachable by all the younger men. She was set apart, as if she was indeed their stepmother. She was the centre of the house, the *primum mobile*. It all radiated from her, and all flowed back to her again. She wielded it unconsciously, never made a mistake and had no enemies. If Inveroran had lacked a daughter for fifteen years, it took to the having one by instinct and turned to Helena as a new-born child turns to the breast.

Hector loved her romantically, Wynyard hungrily, Pat gaily, frankly rejoicing in her beauty, grace and charm. Pierpoint, who had conquered her, now that he could not

wear her in his cap, seemed not to love her at
all. She was quite at her ease with him, lec-
tured him about his domestic delinquencies,
tried to get him into activity again—she
wanted him to resume his soldiering, recom-
mended the Turkish service, and so on; but
she certainly saw less of him than of the
others, and I think that was because he didn't
care to see more of her. It was more interesting to see her with the silent, fierce-hearted
Wynyard. Her power with him was marvellous. She alone made him talk; she alone,
by a mere look of those warm, grey eyes of
hers, could quench the angry gleam in his.
It must have been hard work, continual
sword-play on her part; a ceaseless watch,
a ceaseless reminder that she was not for him
and yet all for him. She could have loved
him as he wanted, I don't doubt. I don't
doubt but he knew that. But Wynyard was
a good fellow, and she was a good woman.
She was a beautiful woman, too—much more
beautiful than I remembered her when misery
and boredom had made her haggard. Her
short diet of love had enriched her; as the
poet said, it had "Softened the lines of brow

and breast"—but her beauty, soft and sumpt-
uous as it was, was spiritualized, too. No
Malleson, at any rate, could have hinted a
wrong to her now. For them she was "en-
skied and sainted"—and she had done it
herself. Let that be remembered to her
credit.

She rode to the meeting beside Sir Roderick;
she rode a milk-white pony, and had a dark-
green habit, with a blue scarf wound in and
about her black hair. All the Mallesons were
in full war-gear, of tartan and silver buttons,
and bonnets, each with its eagle's feather.
We wound our way up Glen Oran, and then
over a shoulder of Ben Mor, and along another
by a belt of pines, through which you could
see, far below, a feeder of the Oran like a silver
thread. There are still eagles to be seen in
those empty fastnesses of the red deer. There
was one high overhead when we came out of
the wood and saw the clansmen clustered on
the brow of a hill round about the shaft of
Broken Cross. The chief, who was very
superstitious, threw up his hand when he saw
the bird, and halted us all to see which way

he would fly. He bore off in great easy
circles to the South by West, which was on
our right as we stood. When his course was
certain—after an intense few minutes of
waiting—I heard Wynyard breathe quickly.
through his nose, and Sir Roderick say
"Amen." He had taken the right direction,
then! and we moved on. It was pleasant to
see how gravely Hector lent himself to the
augury, and with what interest Helena herself
flushed and paled as she breathlessly watched.

We were met with a clamour of cheering, of
waving bonnets and strange cries which showed
the spirit of the gathering. Men and boys were
there—few women, few girls. Fine, fiery, enthusiastic faces, bright and keen blue eyes. I well
knew their merits, but had not been prepared
for such ardent support of a questionable cause.
Sir Roderick bared his head to the cheering,
but did not dismount. He sat his pony
throughout, and kept Helena by his side.
In fact, it was Hector alone who took the
floor on his own feet. He stood on the mound
beside the broken shaft, and spoke to the
company in Gaelic. So far as I could judge

—though I have no idea what he said—he
spoke with perfect ease. He was certainly im-
passioned; he fetched up deep murmurs of
assent and at moments wild cries which
seemed to gratify the old chief. I saw him
turn his eyes full of proud tears on the beautiful woman beside him, who sat her horse
so well and looked so calm and noble. At
the close, when Hector swept her into his
speech with an extended hand, a strange
scene followed. They came streaming up the
hill and held out hands, bonnets, crooks and
staves to her. They cried her, I believe, a
daughter of the Malleson nation. As many as
could reach shook her hand. And then Sir
Roderick, swelling with pride, stood up in
his stirrups and shrieked a few well-known
words. They were, no doubt, a slogan, or
war-cry of the clan. They were taken up
with cheer after cheer. The Mallesons were
beset with their kindred. Hector, dangerously
flushed, quite out of himself—Wynyard burning bright; Pierpoint with his handsome
head once more erect and moved; young
Patrick wild as a hawk: they could have had
an army down the glen if they had willed it,

and cleared out the town. Luckily the von
Broderode party did not show up that day, or
there would have been bloodshed. The pipers
struck up and marched round and round the
knoll at a quick step. We saw it out to the end.

Going home, I asked Hector what he had
said to them to make them so wild. He
answered me that it had been nothing dangerous. He had reminded them of the Curse
of the Mallesons, he said, and told them how
it had been removed by the beautiful lady
who had devoted herself to the salvation of
the house. He asked them if they would see
her go back to slavery and misery; he had
pointed their eyes to her tenderness for his
father—he had called on them to testify to
their gratitude. That was all.

He hadn't mentioned the Baron and his
friends!

Pat said to me, "How the old Baron would
have enjoyed that! He *would* have been
excited!" And then he said, as if meditating,
"I don't know—but I don't believe he's half
so bad as Hector makes out."

That was and had always been my own
opinion.

17

It was expected that when the Games were held, as was intended, in the Castle policies, there would be some definite expression of the Town's feeling. It was expected that the Baron's friends would appear and make a demonstration. I don't know how the idea arose; but it pervaded the Castle and the glens. What actually happened was, in its way, much worse for the Trojans—I mean for the Castle.

The Clan turned out in force, as you might expect—though the absence of its women was remarkable. The Castle was there, of course; but Helena was not. None of our ladies went, in fact.

I have a suspicion that the chief was hurt by that. He had got it firmly fixed in his old headpiece that we were the injured party, and was dreadfully apt to look upon that as disloyalty which was only common reticence and decency. As Pat said, "The pater pinches himself in the door and thinks you an enemy in disguise because you don't go about in a finger-stall!" I knew afterwards, as a matter af fact, that they did witness our revels from the bank of the river, where they were not conspicuous to the revellers.

We revelled in the customary manner, without the gaiety of the customary meetings. It was less like an athletic gathering, and much more Homeric in consequence. Pierpoint recovered some of his old prestige by winning the hill-climbing contest in great style. Wynyard tossed the caber and no one could come near him. The rest of the competitions were wisely allowed to the clansmen. In the midst of the broadsword heats I saw the public attention distracted, and looked in the direction of nearly all eyes but mine. The Baron von Broderode, upon a pony—quite unattended—entered the grounds, and surveyed us all from a small eminence. You never saw such an effect as this produced. An electric thrill seemed to pass from body to body. Sir Roderick literally bristled. Hector stiffened and stared at something else. The contestants hacked away for dear life, and, like everybody else, pretended that they were interested in what they were doing. Pat and I were sitting together on a heather bed, and watched what happened. We were both the least bit out of touch with the meeting because of our Baronial sympathies. Not

that we didn't adore Helena with everybody else; but, as Pat said, we could adore
just as much if the Baron was in the house
with her.

He was in no condition to be on horseback.
He poked his head, he swayed about. His
eyes were fixed. He was engaged in a frightful
struggle to be at ease. All at once the pony
stumbled, and he was off. Pat and I raced
to him, and lifted him. He was out of breath
but not at all scared. "Brave fellows, brave
fellows!" he said. "Lift me. I will go back
as I came. I am not at all hurt. It is a rule
of the game that you go on—ha? Lift me to
his back."

Well, we did. The meeting paused in its
breath to watch us. We got him back,
though he was like lead to lift. Directly he
was there, he was all there. His eyes laughed
at us—merry, saucy, bold and unconquerable.
"If all the English were like you," he said,
"the Austrians would never touch you. Have
no fear at all."

Pat said that was all right. And was he
hurt?

"Not at all, not at all," he said. "It is a

rule of the game." I don't know what he meant by that.

"Would you like us to go back with you?" . we asked him.

"No," he said, "I stay here"—He was very quick to notice things. He saw my face fall—"unless you wish me to go?"

I said, "Oh, I think you might go in this instance." He laughed outright.

"That is all I want. Yes, yes. I will go. What you say, I will be clear." He wouldn't let us go down with him—no, no, all went all. Never better. He waved his hand, and turned the pony's head.

We watched him go. "By Jove," Pat said, "he'll beat us. He's a Roman soldier."

What interested me was the flutter of distress from the bank. Helena in her white dress and black sash, signalling with a handkerchief—like Isolda. I went to her. She was in a beautiful agony.

"Tell me, tell me. It is well?" She never named him if she could help it.

"Yes," I said. "He won't be helped. He's as brave as he can be."

She was half sobbing—"Oh, I know, I know! Oh, what shall I do? Was—did you see Teresa?"

I said that there was no Teresa—but that she was probably hovering somewhere.

Then she said, "You must go and enquire —soon—soon. Promise me you will go."

I said, "Will you come with me?"

She stopped. She looked down, blushing. I do believe she wanted to go. "No," she said, "I cannot go now. I must ask Sir Roderick. He might be angry with me."

I said, "Oh, he would—" then I promised that I would go, and left her. She dried her eyes and turned to join the other ladies. Old Laura Bacchus lost none of the play. I saw Sir Roderick trotting over the sward to be with her. It was pretty to see her upturned face, and his down-turned. He patted her cheek, and she stood by his knee meekly to watch the games.

I judged my time, and when they were busy over the prize-giving, which Helena began to do very charmingly under the chief's approving gaze, I went down into the town.

A few curious looks were cast at me, but of course I was, comparatively speaking, a stranger in Inveroran. Intercourse with the town had never been the thing for the Castle people. The painting at Rosemount seemed to be finished, but no furnishing had been as yet attempted. I went into the Marine Hotel and asked for the Baron. A page-boy tiptoed away, as if we were going to be shown the San Graal, and I followed. He was bestowed on the ground floor, I noticed. We passed his bath-chair in the passage.

I found him in a window of ample bows, a window which gave on to the garden and a flagstaff, dressed for dinner and in the company of his friends. He received me with a cheer. "Ah, brava, brava!" he said. "Here we hef another Ambassador from the proud enemy." He laughed away any possible enmity there might be in his words. The room was full of cigar-smoke, bottles of Rhenish were on the table, long glasses, syphons and all such gear. He introduced me to his friends in great style.

"Become acquainted, if you please, with my good friend Count Szombor Jelacics, and my

trusty and well-beloved cousin and councillor
the Freiherr von Ostensee—" and then he
rang out my name.

The tall and cavernous-eyed young man,
the short and round-faced and very pink-and-
flaxen young man bowed from the hips. But
the Baron went on—"And permit me to
introduce to you also my young and sympathetic friend, Mr. Patrick Malleson." He
rolled out this name with a mighty gusto—
and then I saw Master Pat's grin hover
through the murky air.

"Don't play the Cheshire Cat at me,
man," I said. "I didn't guess you were
here."

The Baron stretched out a benevolent hand
and took Pat's arm. "He came because he
was a good fellow," he said. "He knows
that I am not a bad one. And you also"—
this to me—"I will be glad of, if you will
allow me. Now you will smoke with us?
You will drink with us? Pray help yourself.
My friend Patrick has the strong waters of
his country. You will have the same? Very
good—as you please. But if I were to drink
that whisky of yours, in two weeks I should

be dead, and the flag at Rosemount halfway down the pole."

In this way he began, and continued to rattle on, drinking in volumes of cigar-smoke with the deepest contentment. You would have said that he hadn't a care in the world. I was, myself, in a conflict all the time, of admiration and pity; for it was impossible not to see the ravages which illness had made upon him. He was yielding, he was bound to yield; but he fought every inch of the way. It would kill him—but all his wounds would be in front.

While Pat was explaining with infinite patience and lost effort the merits of the game of golf to the Freiherr von Ostensee—who received them with a deferential scepticism delightful to witness, I took the opportunity to say to von Broderode that I was indeed an ambassador, as he had suggested at a venture. He heard me with raised eyebrows and twinkling eyes. He heard me, he nodded his head many times, and ended with a great shrug.

"My dear sir," he said at last, "if I do not undertsand women, be sure of one of two things: either I am the greatest fool in the

world, or nobody understands them. Not
only do I accept your word—that is of course
—but I am prepared to understand your word.
When women act from the heart they never
go wrong. When they act from the head they
always do, because they think of so many
things at once. Now men—and you will
allow me to call myself a man—think of only
one thing at a time. And they think with
head and heart together. And they have a
will-power which is the servant of both. Not
so with women. Their will-power is only at
the service of the heart. Unless they are mad!
And my wife is not mad. Not at all—not at
all. She is a woman through and through."

I thought that he was right, though I said
nothing. He ended up in this fashion, and
with a request:

"Your friend Hector is a dangerous man,
because he is a man-and-woman. It is so.
He is hermaphrodite. With the heart of a
woman and the brain of a man, he has the
will-power added, of a man-woman. His
will-power is at service of heart or brain. He
puts it here to the work of both. He will fail
—but he does not know it. He does not

intend to fail. Now do me the kindness to
bring him here. To-morrow my friends will
be gone. There is nothing for them to do
here. I do not need them. I am sufficient.
They are good fellows—I like them; but
they want to fight with your men—and that
is absurd. Your red Wynyard would smash
them both like oxen. And then he would be
transported or hanged. What good is that
to me? No! I send them away to-morrow
in the *Coryphæus*, and I stay here for Rosemount to be ready. Already the furniture is
on the way. In a week, two weeks, I shall be
happy to see you there. We will play piquet
together—and talk of politics and history.
But bring the hermaphrodite, the dangerous
.man. Oblige me."

I got up and shook hands. Pat came with
me. As we went up the hill he said, "We
shall be called traitors. The pater will be
very sick."

"I was sent down," I told him. He looked
grave.

"Oh, that's it, is it? I suspected as much."
Then he said "Poor old pater!"

XIX

THE AMAZEMENT OF HECTOR

WE were late home, with barely time to dress; but she lay in wait for me and caught me just as I was about to clear the steps. She came out of the little ante-room, dressed in gauzy black—which made her look her favourite part of the moon clear of clouds. A soft and yet keen persistence in her manner heightened the comparison. She was remote, she was cold; yet she was searching.

"Well," she said, "so you went down? And what do you bring back?"

"He was glad to see me. He called me Ambassador—Ambassador from the proud enemy."

Her eyes fell. She seemed to be looking at her own fairness. "I am not proud," she said.

"You would have excuse if you were," I said. She looked out into the dusk.

"I am not at all proud. I am very much distracted."

"The Baron wants to see Hector," I told her.

268

She opened her eyes. "Hector? Why Hector?"

I said, "Well, Hector is not head of the house, of course; but I suppose he could not expect the chief to go."

She shivered. "Oh, no. Sir Roderick would not go."

I said, "Will you ask Hector to go?" She thought that over.

Presently she said, "No—I cannot. Shall you ask him?"

"Do you mean 'Will I ask him?'"

"I wondered whether you would. I wondered what you thought," she said, avoiding my question.

I said, "I'll ask him, if you wish it?"

Her words almost caressed me. "I think you know best. I think you will do what is best."

I excused myself then. "I really must go and dress. I'm in hot water as it is, I don't doubt. If I'm late as well as a traitor, I shall be boiled before I've done."

She said gently, "You are not a traitor. You are kind. You wish to do the best thing."

"So do you," I said. "I know it." Her eyes appealed; a sad smile faltered about her parted

lips. It was like sunshine in late autumn, pale
and flickering, soon gone. And then I left her.

Sir Roderick made no inquiries after his
enemy; but Wynyard asked me how he was.

"I'm glad you went," he said, when I had
told him about the Baron's gallantry. "I
should have gone myself if you hadn't."

"I'm glad you didn't," I said. "He has
a hairy friend who wants to fight you."

Wynyard said, "That's rot, of course."

"No," I said, "he means it."

Wynyard said, He had better wait till there
was something to fight about, because when
that occurred there would be nobody here to
fight with. That was the nearest Wynyard ever
went to admitting that it would be good to run
away with Helena. I am sure that he had
never hinted at such a thing to herself. But I
daresay that she knew all about it, all the same.

Hector agreed to see the Baron. He made
no difficulty about it. "I am perfectly willing to see him, but I hope he understands
that I don't desire it. I shan't conceal my
opinion of his conduct, of course."

"I expect that he has his own ideas about

that," I said, "and honestly, my dear chap, you'll find him a hard nut to crack."

He gloomily accepted that.

I thought I had better say one thing more. "His case is that, between you, you have induced his wife to desert him. His strong impression is that it was you who did it."

"He's wrong," Hector said. "I am very glad that she did it, but it wasn't my doing."

"My dear man!" I said. "You fell in love with her at Gironeggio."

"I did. Immediately."

"And she knew that."

"Probably."

"That made her dissatisfied with her lot."

"Good Heavens!" said Hector, "If it did that it was worth it."

"Then she came here, and you all fell in love with her."

"Well?"

"Then you brought her back here."

"Well?"

"That's the Baron's case," I said.

He replied stiffly to that, that the Baron had a good advocate. I was unable to deny that I was, at the moment, very much on his

side—though when we went after the others
into the drawing-room, and I saw her the
centre of a pretty group about the fire, I
confess that my heart was open to the pity
of it. They were so unfeignedly happy, there
was such a cosy look about them. Here was
the very emblem of home. Old Sir Roderick
sat in his elbow-chair, his first supporting his
head. The other hand was on Helena's hair.
She sat on a stool below him and was reading
to him in a low voice. Near her Pat lay
back in an easy-chair. His hands were clasped
behind his head, his eyes were fixed on the
ceiling. He made a long straight line from
his chin to his toes. He listened, he smiled.
Pierpoint was watching her from the other
corner. Wynyard, as usual, stood to listen.
He was like the sentinel flamingo, watchful,
on one leg, while the others feed on the sea-
flats. Miss Bacchus was playing patience by
herself, but with a caustic comment now and
then for what she overheard. "Silly ass!
What on earth did he do that for?" I heard
as I shut the door. The book was "The
Earthly Paradise," and the tale concerned
Gudrun and her criss-cross love-affairs. It

was a pretty group, and as snug as Christmas. I thought of the Baron, with his liqueur and his cigar, his avid, wayward hands and his daring blue eyes. I thought of her alone with him, without an intimate word to say. I saw what Hector had seen at once with his diviner's eye and his tentacles at work. I said to myself. "You pretty, gentle creature, what mercy did they show you who taught you their comforts?" And at the moment I felt that if anything could be done to save her from her portion I could do it.

Hector and I went down to see the Baron. It was a fine afternoon, and he received us in the garden of the hotel. The moment we appeared he waved his hand to me. Then he took off his Homburg hat. That was for Hector's benefit. He did not offer to shake hands; but that was the only sign of enmity he showed. Hector was very stiff and solemn, which I thought was a pity. The Baron was perfectly at ease.

He began: "I have wished to see you because I have something to say to you. I should have written to you myself; I should

18

have said, My dear sir, come and see me!
We will have a few words together in private.
It would have been better in private—what
I have to say. For me, I don't mind; but
for you it would be better. . . . .

"But you would not have come. You
have your own idea of me. You think I
am a savage. You think I tear and mangle.
You would say to yourself, I will have no
dealings with the wicked. So you shall hear
what I have to say in the presence of your
friend. . . .

"It is not the first time that your nation
goes to work teaching people their own business. You see me at Gironeggio. You say,
Here is a wicked man. His hand shakes;
he is not like me. He smokes many cigars;
I don't like cigars. He enjoys himself: that
is bad. You see my wife; you like her.
You say, She is a beautiful woman. I could
make her happy—she would be happy with
me. To see her with that old savage makes
me unhappy. Therefore, you say, it makes
her also unhappy. Then you make her
acquaintance and you tell her how unhappy
she is. That is why I call you the dangerous

man. You are dangerous because you see
what you think you see, and you teach other
people your disastrous wisdom! . . .

"You see only yourself, my dear sir. That
is your little mistake. In my wife you see
yourself unhappy. In myself you see yourself
a fool. You think me a fool, but I am not
at all a fool. I am a sensible man because
I know what I want."

He sat there rosy and twinkling, a spectacle
of weather-worn strength, his terrible hands
flickering as he held cigar and match. He
bent his head forward and looked out over
his gold-rimmed glasses, as he said these
words: "I shall win in the end, you will see,
because I have nothing else to do. I shall
get what I want. It is my career. I am not
likely to make a mess of that. You have
youth and good health and your family behind
you to make you strong. But I, my good
sir, have ennui. I must beat that or it will
kill me. And I do not intend to die. Do
you not see that?"

I knew he was speaking the truth. To my
mind he was unanswerable, and it it the fact
that Hector had no answer for him. He sat stiff

in his chair for a little time. Then he got up,
murmured a few inaudible words, and went out.

There was nothing for me to do but follow
him.

He was silent for the length of our walk
up the main street. When we got within
sight of the gates he stopped.

He lifted his head. "I shall fight him."
he said. "If I die for it I'll fight him. For
it comes to this, that a man can possess a
woman's body and soul if he is only cruel
enough. If I took Helena away and made
myself master of her I should beat him. It
is because I will not degrade her in the eyes
of the world that he beats *me*. But he shall
not. I'll fight him for her."

I saw that he was very much moved, and
did not care to argue with him. What I did
say was that the thing ought to be put squarely
before her. It was a case for a woman, I
said. Let Laura Bacchus have it out with
her. Put her to work. He pished, and said,
"Damn Laura Bacchus."

But I was nearly right. It was a case for
a woman; but Laura Bacchus was not she.

XX

PIERPOINT

I HAD had my eye on Pierpoint for some time.
Love was awake and walking in his breast
again. He was like Hector in that, that he
was always in love with somebody; but unlike
him in that his love couldn't live on air. He
must reassure himself with testimonies; he
must wear a gage.

I watched him, not without amusement, to
see how wary he was. He had need to be,
for Wynyard was mortally jealous of him.
Those two never spoke to each other by any
chance. At the best of times they had had
little to say to each other; but since Helena
had been here the same room could hardly
contain them.

There were few, if any, overt acts. I guessed
at what was going on by the recrudescence of
the conquering hero about Pierpoint. His
moustaches took an upward twist; his clothes
were more *soignés,* his neckties, the tops of
his stockings were more carefully contrasted.

He talked to Helena again—upon carefully
impersonal topics, but if you were interested
enough to be careful you could detect a
stream of tendency, an implication. Sometimes there was a complete double sense to
what he said, to which, when once you got a
clue, you must needs devote yourself body
and soul. And he did it pretty well. I fancy
he was enormously pleased with himself. He
flattered himself that Helena was completely
instructed, and Wynyard completely in the
dark; whereas I am sure that it was just the
other way. Helena was a fairly simple character—as simple as a thoroughly pretty and
thoroughly petted woman can be. She was,
of course, petted all round, and she loved it;
but she took it quite innocently. I don't
believe she wanted to marry any of those
chaps, though at the same time I believe that
she would have married any one of them who
asked her—except Hector. She was rather
afraid of Hector. His ideas of love were too
fearful and wonderful for her. While they
were new they would have depressed her,
when they were familiar they would have
bored her. I think she saw all that from the

beginning. But any one of the others would have done. She didn't want anything of a husband but petting; and as she was being petted to her heart's content at this time she didn't want a husband at all.

But Wynyard was altogether different. He wanted her dreadfully. This need had changed the whole habit of the man. It had made him morbidly suspicious, morbidly acute. His passion was driven inwards, it had to feed upon his own vital juices. He had never been a communicative man. He was only really open with his dog, and with the wild creatures which he pursued so remorselessly and killed with such art. I could very well imagine him telling the spirits of the wind and the rain of his hopeless trouble and his infinite desires. They were infinite because Helena could never have given him all he wanted; they were hopeless because he knew it. But she drew him in and in, he flickered and flacked about her pale flame. He was scorched and maimed but he stayed on. The one immediate resource he had—and that was a savage one—was in watching his brother Pierpoint. He hated him; and Pierpoint

seemed to know it and to snatch a fearful joy
in outwatching and outmarching him.

Laura Bacchus was convinced that there
would be bloodshed. She said that she couldn't
rest in her bed until she knew that these
two were safely in theirs. Almost every night,
she told me, she crept out into the corridor,
flitted along it and stole upstairs to the next—
to listen. She used to carry her candle, and
when it showed up Vixen's green eyes, she
knew the bitch was on her master's door-
mat, and that all was well. That's what she
told me, after the event. For there was an
event, and it came suddenly, and soon.

I don't know whether it was a week, or
more, or less, after Hector's and my visit to
the Baron. More than a week, I think,
because Rosemount was furnished, and the
Baron installed when next we saw him. He
had been at one of his bow windows, and
waved his cigar-hand to us as we passed.
Some people had come to stay at the Castle
—Mrs. Muir and her two girls, Elspeth and
Grizel, were there on their way further North;
and a young friend of Pat's, a nice boy called

Chesilworth. They were very good for us, made us brisker, and gave the servants more to do. We used to dance in the evenings, and this gave Pierpoint his chance, and made Hector sad, and Wynyard furious. Neither of those two were dancers.

Pierpoint, having done his duty by the Muir girls—with a dance apiece—spent, and proposed to go on spending, the rest of this opportunity with Helena. He was a wonderful dancer, and naturally she liked it. The first night Wynyard stood it; the second night he got through a bit of it, but then disappeared, and no one knew where he was. The third night there was no dancing at the house, because we all went down to dine upon a cruiser that had come into the bay. We dined and danced there, and Wynyard could stand that because Pierpoint was one of many, and of very little account at that. Helena, with a capricious twist to her head, chose to dance hardly at all that night. She stood mostly by the chief, and danced square dances with the Captain and the Commander. Indeed, poor Wynyard got a bit of an innings, for one of the lieutenants was a friend of his, and was presented by him to Helena. The three of them sat out for a dance or two, which must have been very jolly for the lieutenant, I should say. However, he was a good sort.

The next night there was trouble. Pierpoint himself urged for dancing, and got it. This time Wynyard went out on to the terrace and padded up and down like a native with the toothache. After a time I joined him and we paced up and down together under the stars of one of the most beautiful September nights I ever remember.

I don't know how long we had been there when we saw a white dress glimmering away from us. I didn't need the quick short gasp from Wynyard to know who it was. It was Helena, of course. She had slipped out through the little side door which gives from the ante-room on to the terrace. She was alone, as we saw; but she was not to be alone for long. Wynyard left me to go after her, and had just reached the door from which she had come when that opened again and Pierpoint blundered out almost upon his brother.

Wynyard turned, and they stood facing each other. Neither of them spoke for quite a perceptible time.

Then Pierpoint said "Where's Helena?"

Wynyard—I could hear his pumps at work—answered, "She's in the garden."

"Oh," said Pierpoint, "that's all right," and made a move.

Wynyard said, "Stay where you are."

Pierpoint had no answer at the moment; then said breathlessly, "What on earth do you mean?"

"What I say," Wynyard replied. "You will stay where you are, or go in."

"It's not for you to tell me where I'm to go."

"In this case it is."

A third figure came to the door and stood in the light of it. It was Ethel Cook, with a silvery cloak for Helena.

"Go back with your wife, you dog," said Wynyard; and left him facing the girl.

She shuddered and shrank against the door as if someone was going to hit her. I saw her mouth open. Her eyes were hidden in the shadow of their own brows. "I never told him—I swear I didn't," she said in short gasping breaths. But he left her and walked past me to the other side of the house. She stood looking out into the dark. Her mouth was still open. I thought she was going to faint, and went to her.

"Ethel," I said, "I heard all this, and am awfully sorry for you."

She was struggling with her tears. "I didn't tell him—I never told a soul," was all she could say.

"No, no," I said. "I'm sure you didn't. Nobody thinks you have done anything wrong. Nobody who knows you would think so."

She had now covered her face in her hands and was crying. "He made me do it— because I wouldn't—because I couldn't——"

"Don't tell me," I said. "I don't want to know. But if you take my advice, you'll tell the Baroness. That will be the best thing in the world." She listened, though she went on crying. I went at her again.

"The Baroness is very fond of you. She knows what you are thought about up here. She has troubles of her own, as you and I know. Well, if you tell her your story, you'll

help her as much as she'll help you. So do you
take my advice, and when she goes upstairs,
tell her all about it. You needn't be afraid
of Mr. Wynyard. *He* won't tell her. I'll
answer for that."

She had stopped crying. She was thinking.
Then she said, "I never told anybody because
I didn't want to make mischief. I'd have put
up with almost anything. I *have* put up
with a good deal—but I couldn't hurt Sir
Roderick—not if I was driven out."

"You won't hurt Sir Roderick by telling
the Baroness. I promise you that," I said.

"No," said Ethel. I know that. He'll
take almost anything from her." I could
see that she was convinced. Presently she
thanked me and said so.

"It's bound to come out now," she said,
"whatever I do. And I'd rather tell her
myself than have anybody tell against me."
Then she thanked me and went away. Helena
had no cloak that night, and no cavalier.

I went into the smoking-room and got myself a whisky-and-soda. The two boys came
in, Wynyard and Hector together, then Sir
Roderick for his customary dram and a pipe.

I had plenty to think about, and as there
were plenty of them, I had no need to talk.
I don't think that I was astonished at what
I had heard, because Pierpoint was Pierpoint.
He wasn't the sort to stick at a wedding if he
couldn't get what he wanted any other way.
And he would always think that he would
never want to do it again. With your genuine
amorist every affair is for good and all. And,
as he figured it all out, I've no doubt he
thought a secret marriage, with stolen meetings, stolen confidences, stolen pledges of
troth—would be a very romatic affair. As,
no doubt, it was—for him. But the girl
herself made me wonder: how on earth she
had seen what she had seen and kept her
patience and her nerve—that beat me. What
a fine pride to her! What a dignity! Nothing
asked, yet nothing refused. No hope, yet no
despair. And no illusion after the first week.
How could there have been? No, she must
have said to herself, Men are made so, and
women have to give way to them. She must
have had a certain scorn of her scampish
husband, too. I could imagine that short
upper lip of hers curving to her fine nose as

she considered him and caught sight from an upper window—her duster in hand—of his goings-on with fair lady visitors. Yet she was never tempted to shatter his bubbles for him! Never itched to put a hand on his shoulder as he stooped to whisper or entreat —or to shake him with a "Come to me, husband!" No, no. Men were made so, and women must give them their heads. Oh, proud and patient Ethel Cook!

One by one they went to bed, but Wynyard remained. He pulled at his pipe for a while, meditating. He was quieter than he had been for some days.

Presently he stirred, and gave me a steady look. "It came out of me directly I saw her coming," he said. "I was savage and let out. I'm not sorry, except for Ethel. I don't think I ought to have done it—but I let out. I shall go on now I've begun with it. She's a good girl. He shall do the square thing by her now."

"You needn't say anything just yet," I said. "Leave her alone for a bit. She's telling Helena about it. I advised her to."

He stared; then showed relief. "Oh, I'm

glad of that. You were perfectly right.
That's the best thing she can do. Helena
will be kind to her."

"Yes, I know." I agreed with that; but
then I warned him that it would react on
Helena.

"Not a doubt of it," he said. "That
blackguard has been making love to her
again. When I was out in Vienna I warned
him."

"Oh, that was what you did! You let him
know what you knew?" I said.

Wynyard nodded.

"He knew then. I was bound to stop him.
And I did. He kept himself in hand after
that. He has behaved decently here until
lately."

I asked him how he had found out, and he
said it was in a very curious way. Five years
ago he had been in Berwick for a night on his
way to fish with the G——s at Coldstream.
A man—a clergyman, in fact—had come up
behind him where he was standing in front
of a shop window with a "Good evening, Mr.
Hammond," and when he turned about, still
held out a hand. Wynyard had denied the

name, but the man, though more doubtfully, held on to it. "Surely I'm not mistaken," he said. "Surely I married you this time last year?" Wynyard said, "Indeed, he did not;" and the clergyman said, "Well, if it was not you it was your brother." He admitted that the facial likeness was not extraordinary; but from behind, he said, he would have sworn it. Wynyard asked, "Whom did his brother marry?" And the man replied at once, "a Miss Ethel Cook, a handsome young lady."

"Then," said Wynyard, "I thought it was worth looking into. He showed me the Register. *Philip Hammond*, in the fellow's own handwriting, and *Ethel Cook*. By special license, too. Six years ago this August."

"And you kept it to yourself?" I asked him.

"I did," said Wynyard. "We never loved each other, but it was no business of mine."

"What do you suppose he'll do now? Will he face it out?"

Wynyard thought not. "He wouldn't do that. There'd be no fun in it, you see. And again, there'd be no fun out of it. He likes a cake in the cupboard, but he wants any

19

amount on the table, too. I think he'll go abroad."

"And let her rip?"

"Yes. He'll be pretty sure my father will get to know about it. He'll argue it out with himself. He might send for her in a few years' time, when he's had his whack."

"Do you think she'd go?"

"You can't tell. At least I can't. I don't know anything about women."

"The chief will hear of it, no doubt," I said.

He thought so. But it wouldn't be from him, he said.

XXI

SURRENDER

THE man who put out my things said to me as he was going out of the door, "The Baroness' compliments, sir, and she would be glad if she could see you for a moment before breakfast. She will be in the morning-room."

There she was, when I came to look for her, dressed in black, with a red rose in her belt, and another in her hand for the chief. She was pale, but quite composed.

She thanked me for sending Ethel to her. She said it was a great compliment. There was nothing she loved more than being useful.

"I am sure that you were useful to Ethel," I said.

"Yes, I hope so. I kept her with me all night. We were useful to each other. I suppose you know. I suppose you understand that this is a great shock to me."

I said, "No doubt." And there could be no doubt at all. Had she applied the balms of Araby to her unguarded lips? But if I

gathered aright there had been more than
a kiss or two. Wynyard would not have put
the screws on unless there had been urgent
need for it. Pierpoint had beset her, seriously.
She only knew how much need there had been
for them, when Wynyard brought up his
reserves. All this must have been terrible
to the poor lady. Nothing brings a conscience
so sharply to the ache as the conviction that
one had been fool as well as rogue.

I could see that she was, indeed, sore all
over. She said sharply and stiffly, too, "Of
course there is only one thing for me to do."

"Oh, no," I put in, "there are lots of
things for people like you to do."

She stopped, and recovered herself. "What
do you mean?"

I said, "You see, you have the poor girl
to comfort. She must be put right with the
world and herself. Nobody but you can do
that. Nobody here, at least, has such tactful
fingers. Do you want her to weep out her
troubles on the cook's bosom? Or Miss
Bacchus's?"

That steadied her. She softened immediately. "I will do everything for her," she

said. "Indeed, we have talked of that.
She wishes to leave. She has asked to come
with me. I hope she will."

I said, "I don't think Sir Roderick will
like that. He will want to be told the reason."

She looked down. "No," she said, "he
won't. If I go, he'll be glad for her to be
with me." Of course she was right. Ethel
would be a hostage.

She then told me that she should go back
to the Baron to-day or to-morrow. The Muirs
were leaving to-day. It would be to-morrow
then. That would give him twenty-four
hours' notice.

I said something—I don't know what—
about the distress of Inveroran. She said
that she knew that. "They love me, and I
love them. They will be unhappy, and so
shall I. But I have done wrong. I didn't
know it and am not happy at all. You think
me wicked—"

I protested to Heaven. "You do not, because you are kind, or because you understand. Well, I won't be wicked any more.
It is a great pity that one can't be happy
if one is good." Then she held out her hand

to me. She was an innocent, tender creature. I was very much in love with her myself.

At breakfast, Sir Roderick asked where Pierpoint was, but got no answer until Hector came down, rather late. He had a note in his hand which he took over to his father. He stood by him while he read it. Pierpoint said that he had gone South, and wanted his servant to bring him his things. He was sorry he hadn't had time to say good-bye. He would write to his father from London.

Those who were surprised and those who were not surprised didn't show any sign of disturbance. Patrick said he had missed the first decent fishing day we had had. It was true that yesterday's rain had been followed by a frosty night. There would be sea-trout for the asking.

But Sir Roderick was annoyed. He frowned, fiddling the note in his hands.

"He suits himself—he may do as he pleases. I consider it a want of respect to the lady of the house. That's all I have to say." He frowned as he spoke in Helena's direction. She blushed gratefully, and beamed her thanks and deprecation at once. It made her

job no easier, lady of the house for twenty-
four hours longer.

By lunch-time, when the Muirs were off,
everybody concerned knew that Helena was
going except the chief. She chose her own
time for telling him. He had his siesta in
peace, anyhow. Wynyard carried off his personal woes to Oranside, and made the sea-
trout smart for it. Goodly hecatombs of
them were offered up. He didn't appear until
dinner-time. Pat went fishing, too. He
said, "Frightful score for the Baron, I must
say. I don't see why we shouldn't take our
licking in real style and ask him here. I
believe he'd come, too."

I said, "I believe he would if you asked
him, Pat." Pat said that he'd do it for
twopence. Then he said that he thought he
should clear out in the course of the day.
"We shall have an awfully wet night of it
if we don't look out."

Miss Bacchus, I believe, when she was told,
said, "Well, my dear soul, what else could
you do?" or words to that effect. She was
arguing from *a priori* grounds, I suppose,
for it is unlikely that Helena confided Ethel

Cook's scrape to her vigorous treatment. But
certainly Miss Bacchus put two and two
together, for she said to me in her caustic
way, "I suppose the sweet tooth bit on a
peach-stone. That hurts." Then she said
sharply, "Do you think he's gone to London?"

"Who? Pierpoint?" I parried her. "Oh
why not?"

"It's a long way to throw a peach-stone,"
said Miss Bacchus. "It must have hurt."

The Baron, like the gentleman he was,
replied to Helena's intimation of surrender
that he would meet her at Euston, naming the
train. He must also have told her the name
of his hotel, as afterwards appeared. This
was letting Sir Roderick down gently, but it
involved an early departure for Helena on
the morrow. She was a long time closeted
with the old chief, telling him her story.
They came into the hall together when tea
was there. He looked very sick, indeed, but
made the best of. Many an anxious glance
passed from her towards him, and he reassured
her with smiling eyes whenever he caught
the beam of hers. You never know what

women feel about these things. They have
so much more self-possession. Hector, of
course, was told, and had his half-hour of
consolation. Wynyard was prepared, naturally, but I suppose she gave him something.
It was astonishing to me how she managed
all those men.

We all had our work cut out for us that
last night of her escapade; but it went off
pretty well. There was no reading. Pat and
his friend made us all play pool. After that
we had billiard-table cricket, and the boys
got excited and made a noise. She went
round and said her good-byes. She would
go very early in the morning, and nobody
was to get up except Hector.

So she went about and got through with
it. Miss Bacchus had a kiss on each cheek,
Pat had a kiss and gave one; Hector would
be seen later. Wynyard put his hand on her
shoulder and said, "Good-bye, Helena:" her
cheek flickered, but was not kissed. I kissed
her hand, and then she was taken to Sir
Roderick's heart.

He was very much moved, but without
a fuss. He kissed her fondly, and said some-

thing which she answered—inaudibly. Then
she went away; and there was the end, or
what seemed to be the end, of a dream.

Meantime Sir Roderick didn't know that
it was his daughter-in-law who was going as
Helena's maid. He had had her in to his
room, and had made her a little speech in the
presence of his sons. He had made her a
handsome present, and had said how glad
he was that she was to be companion to so
dear a friend as the Baroness von Broderode.
To all of which Ethel Cook had listened with
becoming gravity. She had then had her
hand shaken by everybody in turn and had
retired.

Wynyard caught her up-stairs, he told me,
and had a talk with her. He had not then
told Hector, but he said that when he did,
it was probable that Hector would tell his
father. On his own part he undertook, at
a word from her, to put everything on a
proper footing. She thanked him and said
that she preferred to be as she was. She said
that she wasn't fitted to be Pierpoint's wife,
and was quite contented. That was all, so far.

Hector saw them off in the morning—in

a bitter driving mist of rain and brown leaves.
She had another good-bye with the chief, I
heard; and he was on the steps when she
finally departed. Hector went on with them
in the motor to the junction.

Here, for a time, ended my acquaintance
with the prettiest and most pettable lady I
had ever met. She was fitted to be the
wife of any true man, or, indeed, of any
dozen, for her tact and sweetness of disposition
were such that discordance could not be
where she was. No man could hurt her,
and I don't believe that the Baron ever did,
though his hands maybe were not of the
lightest. If you ask me my candid opinion,
I think she was fairly contented until, in a
momentous hour, Hector saw her unhappy
and persuaded her that she was so. The
Baron had seen that with his usual acumen.
By comparison with Inveroran her life with
a vivacious old invalid may well have been
monotonous; for what woman could resist
a houseful of lovers? And so she may have
found her return an anti-climax. The Baron
was going, fine fighter as he was. A stronger
enemy than Hector had him held. I suspect

that he took to his bed, when he reached it,
and once there, there was no getting out on
this side Phlegethon. Well, he had warmed
both hands, back and front. There were few
phials of pleasure in which he had not dipped.
I suppose he was a horrid old scamp; but I
always liked him. He took things as they
came, and lost neither head, heart nor temper.
If he tyrannized his Helena, I am certain
that he never snarled at her. His appetites
were hearty, his tastes somewhat gross, his
pleasures of the earth. Farewell to him,
from me at least, as a man of courage and
resource.

XXII

PASSION OF SIR RODERICK

I HAVE said already somewhere that Sir
Roderick was a man who proceeded by explo-
sions, like a petrol-engine. A spark kindled
him. A rapid series of puffs and snaps, a
whirring and grinding of cogs, and he was
off: very often upon the top of you. So he
had advanced from youth to maturity, and
thence to eld.

But he was a slow-witted, heavy man, too.
He had his fixed ideas, and was himself fixed
in them. When one of these was disturbed
by outside impact he could at first see only
a wanton outrage by the jostler. It was only
by degrees that he appreciated what might
have caused the collision; that the jostler
might himself have been jostled. And when,
by degrees and degrees, the truth stood bare,
it was quite as likely as not that he would
yield to panic—and do considerable damage.

Put it like this, that his mental apparatus
was like a regiment on the march. All goes
well so long as it covers the miles without

obstacle, to the tap of the drum or the whistling of the ranks. But interruption of routine flurries it—the van is hustled by the rear. The drum-taps are intermittent, the whistling ceases. All at once somebody cries out, "*Nous sommes trahis!*" and everybody begins to shoot.

So it was with Sir Roderick. He believed himself supreme in his house; he believed that he pushed that which really pushed him. The household routine went on, and he with it. He believed he was taking a great deal of exercise, he took for granted a vast amount of homage and gratitude from dutiful sons and adoring servants. He pictured the boys pausing in their daily round of sport or fun to look at each other and say, 'God bless the dear old chief for all he is doing for us!' He saw himself as a benevolent despot; and when he found out that he was nothing of the sort—well, he got very cross, and, as I say, did a great deal of damage to himself and others.

When I came down to breakfast on the morning of Helena's departure I was met at the door by Pat and his young friend.

They were tiptoe for a flight. Pat, meeting me, rounded his eyes and pulled his mouth sideways. He durst not say anything or stay his retreat.

I went in, and saw Wynyard alone at the table, red in the face, looking steadily at his father, who stood with a letter in his hand. I turned to fly, but was too late.

The chief was on me. He wheeled round and I saw the fire in his dark-blue eyes.

"Don't leave us—there is no need for that. I think, indeed, that you may be able to move Wynyard's tongue. My son's tongue, sir, which won't wag for his father." He held me out the letter. "Be pleased to read that, sir, and to understand what kind of children I have reared—to disgrace me, by God."

I held the letter in my hand. I said, "Do you really want me to read this?"

Sir Roderick was now solemnly inclined upon his course. "You will oblige me."

It was from Pierpoint.

"MY DEAR FATHER,—You have no doubt heard from Hector or Wynyard, or both, of my leaving Inveroran, and the reason of it,

or what they suppose the reason of it is. I
don't trust to their sympathy, and don't
particularly want it; but I should like you
to know my own account. I left at once
because it seemed the kindest thing to the
persons involved. I have written to my wife
to desire her to join me here, where I have
made arrangements for her establishment.
When you are alone and willing to see me I
will come up and give you full particulars.
But I definitely decline to meet Wynyard,
who had reasons of his own for the course he
took, and lost his head as well as his manners.

> "Your affectionate son,
> "P. G. M. MALLESON.

"P.S.—I propose to live abroad and hope
to get into the Turkish service."

He wrote from an address in London.

I handed the letter back under the glare
of Sir Roderick's eyes.

"Well, sir," said he, "what have you to
say?"

That was a little too much for me. "I
have nothing to say," I answered, "and don't

know what you expect me to say. I had
nothing to do with Pierpoint's marriage, if
you mean that."

He shook the letter at me. "But you
knew of it. You knew that he had a wife—
here—in this house——"

"He doesn't say that," I said rather
foolishly.

"You prevaricate, sir, She was in this
house. She was one of my own servants.
And you knew it."

I didn't know what on earth to do. He
was so angry that I should have made him
worse whatever I said. Wynyard cut in to
the rescue.

"He knew it because it was burst upon
him. He knew nothing of it until then.
He heard me mention it. He was with me
at the time. It was not for him to tell you.
It was for Pierpoint or me." That turned
him blazing on Wynyard.

"And why the devil did you keep me in
the dark, sir? Who are you to say what I
am to hear and what not hear?"

"Well," said Wynyard slowly, "I am not
the husband of the lady, anyhow."

20

Sir Roderick laid hands upon himself. If he hadn't Wynyard would have felt his grip. He became dangerously calm.

"Have the goodness to tell me why you mentioned it, as you are pleased to say, when you did."

Wynyard flushed again.

"I regret it. I should not. But I don't want to drag personal matters into discussion."

"You decline to answer my question?" Sir Roderick said, still very quiet.

"Yes," Wynyard said, "I do."

Sir Roderick paused, as it seemed to me, in the very act to spring. But I suppose that even he recognized that there are limits to the authority of fathers, chieftains though they be. He glared, his mouth was open, he showed his fine teeth—marvellous teeth for a man of his age—but he left Wynyard alone, and turned to the bell-rope. That he tugged at, and stood by it, with his hand still grasping it, until it was answered.

"Ask Mr. Malleson to come to me when he returns," he told the man. Then he stalked out of the room.

"This is beastly," Wynyard said. "It's my fault. I'm sorry."

I said, "He'll find it out, you know. You can't keep Helena out of it."

"Who'll tell him?" said Wynyard.

I said, "My dear man, it's easy enough. He'll guess it."

And of course he did; but it took time. He wrote Helena and had a telegram in reply. Upon that he went to town, and saw her and Ethel Cook. I had left Inveroran, and had the facts from Hector who came down with his father, but did not return with him. He dined with me soon after the thing which he reported had happened, but not before I had myself had a visit from the chief himself, who wrote for an appointment.

Directly we were face to face he came to me with his hand out. "I ask your pardon, my dear friend, for my vehemence. I was unjust and you bore with me." That was handsome in the old boy.

He went on in a hurry: "You were awkwardly placed. You did what you had to do—and no more. Yes, I was unjust. You could not have taken on yourself to tell me

what you had heard by chance. No, no.
But let me tell you that in what you did do—
when you sent that weeping, deluded, ignorant, wronged girl to her mistress's heart, to
her mistress's arms, you did a charitable, a
fine act, sir. It has touched me—it has drawn
me here."

He was greatly moved. His words choked
him. He blew his nose vigorously with a
red silk handkerchief. I said, "Chief, I did
what you would have done at the moment"—
which was pretty of me, but disingenuous,
because I don't think—and didn't then think
—that he would have done anything of the
kind.

But he took it. "Yes, indeed—I hope
so. God help us all! I have seen Helena.
She has told me—I am humbled by the sense
of her generosity. And I have seen the poor
girl, and think that we understand each
other. Well, I won't keep you. You are
good to bear with the self-reproaches of an
old man. These are evil days for my house.
I don't know where I stand at the moment.
My lovers and friends stand afar off! But
I have broad shoulders, and good friends

yet. I doubt not I shall weather it." And
then he marched out, with the air of the pipes
(I am sure) ringing in his ears.

I must summarize events of which I have
no personal knowledge. Hector kept me
informed. Pierpoint was got into the Turkish
Army by interest, and went off without seeing
his father or any of his brothers except
Hector. Hector insisted on an interview and
saw him off. I think he felt it his duty. He
was very strict about that. His Ethel didn't
go with him, and wouldn't see him; but
she admitted, under pressure, that she might
change her mind by and by. She refused
also to be set up by the family, preferring to
be with Helena. Whether that was Helena's
doing I don't know, but suspect that it was.
She had very coaxing ways, and may have
wanted a confidant. And there's another
thing. Helena was exceedingly sensitive to
opinion, and one of the cleverest women I
ever knew at hitting off the right line. She
may well have known how much comfort
her friends at Inveroran would derive from
her keeping Ethel by her. That they were

comforted was beyond question. Hector said
so. He said that the chief couldn't say kind
enough things about Ethel. He was greatly
touched—he hinted at generosities on a large
scale in his will. That proves how clever
Helena was—one mass of tentacles. As for
my poor tentacular friend himself, consumed
as he was by cares for what might or might
not be Helena's fate, resumed by the claws
of her husband, whom his dark imagination
pictured as a horrible cross between Pan,
Priapus, and Mephistopheles, his whole trust
was in the gravity and deep bosom of his
handsome sister-in-law. He made a kind of
Demeter of that fine girl, and pictured her
keeping watch and ward while his pale Perse-
phone shivered in the house of Hades.

The von Broderodes went back to Vienna.
Hector wrote to her once a week, and heard
from her, perhaps, once a month. He showed
me some of her letters, or read me parts of
them. She didn't complain, never mentioned
the Baron (an old trick of hers), said that she
had Hermione at home and seemed happy in
feeling that she was bringing her up properly.
Hermione was getting on for thirteen, a tall

child. She had sent her photograph to Sir
Roderick, and, as I gathered, a good deal
more besides. "I told your father," or "the
chief will know by this time"—constant
phrases in her letters—pointed to a pretty
regular correspondence with the head of the
clan Malleson. But Hector, "the dangerous
man," was not at all dangerous now. He
loved her in his melancholy way. But there
was to be no fruit. It had miffed-off, as the
gardeners say. It was his career, in matters
of the heart, to love romantically, and be
esteemed in return. Like the Austrian Army,
he had a "tradition of defeat." Poor, excellent, chaste Hector.

XXIII

THE END OF IT ALL

WYNYARD went abroad, bought land in Florida, and prospered. He was out there when the news came that the Baron was dead. That was two years, rather more, after he carried home his Helena with such triumph as pertained. Hector dined with me when he had the news, and told me all about it. He said that he had wired to his father, not because it was necessary, for almost certainly Helena had told him, but for an odd reason. "My father likes little attentions, and doesn't like it to be known that he does. So I showed him one on my own account, and led him to infer that I knew nothing of Helena's. Do you see?" He thought that rather neat.

He talked a good deal about her, wondering how she was left off; what she would do with the Galicia estate, with Hermione—and with Ethel. That young woman had not yet claimed conjugal relationship with Pierpoint.

312

Malleson Bey he was now. He had done very
well with a Macedonian rising; was thought
to be a coming man. "If I go out to Vienna,"
he said musingly, "I shall try to arrange
something. It's pretty bad to have a pretty
sister-in-law whom you can't treat as such."

"But you can treat her as such perfectly
well," I told him. "Do you suppose Helena
has left her where she picked her up? Not a
bit of it. I bet you something handsome that
Mrs. Ethel is a somebody in Vienna."

"She'd be a nobody at Inveroran," he said,
"to the end of the chapter. Why, old Sandars
knew her as a between-maid."

"Oh, you can't have her there, of course."
That I admitted. "But you can set her up
with a household."

"I'll see about it," he said, and grew gloomy.
I knew he was thinking of his chances with
Helena, trying to get himself to admit that
they were nothing at all.

But he didn't go out for a long time. He
had heard the news in the summer. In
August he went home and saw his father. No
doubt that they talked about it. I know
that he went with the intention of telling him

what he hoped for. He stayed up there for
his usual time, came back to London in October, and then told me that he was going to
ask Helena to marry him. He was very
.depressed about it.

"I've loved her for nearly four years," he
said. "I feel very nervous. She means so
much to me by this time that I hardly dare
consider her in such a relationship. Don't
you understand that a man may magnify and
enhance a woman so much by constantly
brooding upon her with adoration that the
other feelings are atrophied, as it were?"

I said that I did understand it, but added
that I understood also that atrophy of the
other feelings did not make marriage a hopeful
adventure.

He knew that. He began, "You think
that a platonic union—" and I must needs
laugh.

"Helena is no platonist," I said. "But,
after all, I don't suppose that you are, either.
Nor have you any business to be. The Inveroran nurseries must be filled. You have an
inheritance to hand on."

"Nigel has half-a-dozen children," he said.

"They won't console your wife, my poor Hector," I told him.

He said, It was very difficult. I replied that I understood it was not. But he frowned me down.

The Baron, by his will, had left Rosemount to—Sir Roderick! Posthumous magnanimity, which impressed Hector very much. I hadn't understood before that it had been his own property; but it seems that he bought it outright of Peter Grant: and now, with a cynical twist quite in keeping with his character, had dished that enemy of the Clan Malleson. I could imagine him chuckling as he flapped his spectral wings over the family vault. Hector said that his father would accept the disposition, and was very glad of it, indeed, though he would not allow any merit to the disposer. There had been some question, he told me, whether or not the chief should go out to Vienna, but he had decided that Hector should take his place. Ample provision was to be made for Mrs. Pierpoint; Pierpoint himself was to be urged to proper behaviour. As for Helena, the chief had written to her, no doubt; but Hector had no direct message

to her from the head of his house. The chief
had said to him, "She knows that her home
is here. She'll find the fire on the hearth
whenever she comes, whether it's mine or
yours." That was all he had said, but he
knew that the proud old chap was hungry for
her. "He seems to be waiting. He's always
looking South-east," he said. "And certainly
the place is horribly empty without her."

"Well, my dear man," I said, "it's up to
you. She'll come if you ask her."

He was still very depressed. "One can't
marry to please one's father, you know."

"One doesn't," I said. Then I added,
"Look here, Hector. I won't stand in your
way. I never have yet. But if *you* don't ask
her, I shall."

He was greatly surprised. "You! You
love her?"

I said, "Not in your way. But I like to be
comfortable as much as anybody, and she'd
make any man comfortable."

"Your view is hateful to me," he said—and
he looked it.

I said, "If the thought of her arms don't
inspire you with feelings of comfort, you had

better leave her alone. What! Are you a man,
or an idea? She at least is woman," I said.
"I promise you that." On that he left me.

We parted good friends; for I saw him off
to the East and wished him well. I knew
quite well what was going to happen to him,
and I think he did, too.

It was very like Hector to change his plans
half-way towards the fulfilment of them. He
was ostensibly going to Constantinople. He
went, in fact, directly to Vienna, and I heard
from him there; a short and terse communi-
cation which, I have no doubt, he thought a
business letter.

"Helena is well," he wrote. "A beautiful
serenity upon her, like a silver light on the
sea. Hermione is exactly like her, but colder.
Not so affectionate. Mother and daughter
seem like sisters. I hardly knew Ethel again.
She is a very distinguished person. Willing
to see P., from whom she has had two or three
letters. My father has written to her with
his proposal for her establishment. She is
indifferent to money, but, I think, wants a
child. I hasten to say that this is pure infer-
ence on my part. She looks older than Helena,

to whom she is devoted. She has not been
converted. Helena talks much of Scotland.
I am hopeful of bringing her over in the spring.
The Galician estates are to be sold. They are
Hermione's. Helena has very little. I am
going to Constantinople next week. Helena
does not wish P. to come here—but there is
no likelihood of it. I hear that they think
much of him at Constantinople."

Then he sent me a line from Constantinople.

"P. lives in great style here. He has a kind
of kiosque—rather like a good sort of Floren-
tine villa stuck out in a Venetian lagoon.
Cypresses all about it, a flaky wall with battle-
ments, and weedy steps down into the water.
He wasn't cordial, but heard what I had to
say. My impression was that he would be
glad to have Ethel if he were sure that she
wanted to come. I told him that she was
admired. He said that she always had been,
but that she had been faithful to him in one
class, and no doubt would continue so in
another. I said plainly that he at least had
given her no reason to be so. He answered,
No; but she had had the reason in herself.

That was rather sublime. At the end he said that he didn't care to have her here as his official wife, and I then discovered that he proposed to begin from the beginning. He was for a wooing. It was left like this, that she should settle herself in Vienna, and receive him when he presented himself. He would not, he said, be able to leave his duty for a month or two. If Helena has not gone by that time I shall have to ask her to receive him. I don't think she will desert Ethel until something is fixed. She is very faithful."

He was right. Helena said that the wooing must be done in her house, and that she would receive Pierpoint if he came out to Vienna. She sent Hector home with a message for his father that she charged herself with the duty and would see it through. So far as I could make out, no tender proposals had been made her by my transcendental friend.

There the affair, so far as I was concerned, rested until the summer, when Helena was expected in London, *en route* for Inveroran. Meantime, however, Wynyard had come back to England. He arrived in May.

He looked abundantly healthy, but was
grimmer than ever. Things had prospered
with him. He grew oranges, and sold them.
Had a large property and was adding to it.
But he hadn't come over to deal in oranges.
He told me in so many words that if he could
get Helena he intended to do it. He squared
his jaw, showed angry lights in his blue eyes,
and looked formidable—but yet I doubted.
He might frighten her into it, but the chances
were that he would overdo it. He would not
go North to see his father at present. He said
that he had heard that Helena was coming
to England, and should wait for her. He
hoped to catch her in Paris and make his
cast there. According as he sped, Inveroran should be his next move—or the White
Star home.

He went off accordingly to Paris, and I
didn't hear from him again. I gather that
he made her a definite offer of his heart, hand
and oranges, which she neither accepted nor
rejected, but left in suspense. I gather as
much because he didn't come back with her,
nor cross the Atlantic, but went off walking
by himself in the Pyrenees. He was expected

at Inveroran in the autumn—to learn his
fate—no doubt.

In London she was met by Hector, shining
bolt in hand. He had screwed himself up;
but when or where he sped it I don't know.
Kew Gardens, I believe. The result, in his
case also, was neither hit nor miss. He told
me that she had been very kind to him—and
you know what that means. There had been
tears in her beautiful eyes; but she could
give him no other answer but the assurance of
her gratitude—at present. Hermione and she
were staying with Mrs. Jack Chevenix. I was
asked to meet them, but couldn't go. Pierpoint, I heard, had been in Vienna, and had
laid siege to the heart of his wife, who had
made him the happiest of men. So *that* was
all right, or we were agreed to suppose it so.
Then Helena and Hermione went up to
Inveroran, and Hector was their escort. Then
a bomb burst.

Wynyard came to my rooms one night
while I was at dinner. It was late in July;
London tired, dry and hot. I heard the door
open and a bag flung down in the passage.
I heard Wynyard say, "I shan't keep him a

minute." And then he walked in. The light
seemed to dazzle him. His eyes looked pale,
his mouth was open; he kept opening and
shutting his hands. I pictured him as having
been stuck in a railway carriage all the way
from Pampluna, with his mouth open, and
his hands opening and shutting.

I got up, but he motioned me down.

"Go on," he said. "I'm not going to stay.
I'm heading for Liverpool. I'm off."

"She won't have you?" I said.

He jerked his head. "She can't. She's
going to be my stepmother. God of Life and
Death!"

I wasn't at all surprised, but I had to
pretend to be.

"Droit de Seigneur," I said. "After all, a
chieftain's a chieftain."

Wynyard poured himself out a glass of
sherry."

"I've been a d——d fool. I never thought
of it. My idea was that Hector would ask
her."

"Hector!" I cried. "Not a chance of
Hector." Then I said, "If you really want
my opinion, I think the best man has won.

Your father has no peers. He will give you half-a-dozen young brothers and sisters, and spoil Helena over her pretty head and ears."

Wynyard squared his jaw. "I shouldn't have spoiled her," he said, "nor she me. We should have done very well."

He would have dragooned her; she would have been his slave. But I daresay she would have taken him if he had insisted on it, in time. I have always said of her from the beginning that she would have married any one of them and made him perfectly happy. The best man got her.

Old Laura Bacchus, who was there at the time and saw it all, gave me a detailed account of it. "I always expected it," she said, "at the back of my head. It lay there, put by like a Paisley shawl. I used to look at it now and then and say, 'You wait. I shall find use for you one of these days.' Directly she came up I saw how it was to be. Not from *him*, mind you. You don't catch a Scotchman letting you know his mind. He! He took it as quietly as you please. Didn't go to the station even. Met her on the *perron* and gave her a kiss as if she was his daughter-in-law; and a kiss for young Miss, too, who was shy. No, it was from her I saw what was going to happen. Why, my dear man, she settled down into his arms with a sigh you could hear across the room, fluffing out her breast-feathers like a nesting dove. And croon! My wig, I should think she *did* croon. Just one or two."

"Miss Bacchus, Miss Bacchus," I said, "no poetry here, I beg. Tell me the facts, and I'll work the poetry in afterwards."

"She came," said Miss Bacchus, "with bright fever in her eyes; but that all went after the first day. And she took up her house-keeping where she left it off. The old chief had to blow his nose, the morning he came down and found his rose on his plate. . . You'll see. She'll get plump. She takes it all as a cat laps cream. You can see her lick her whiskers. She sits sleeking herself."

"My friend, my friend!"

"Oh, well," said Miss Bacchus, "I don't see why she should get off. You've always got to pay for your fun. She owes me a lot. . . . Well, it didn't take 'em long. She came to me one afternoon with a soft light in her eyes.

Came gliding in. They had a black-velvety
look, as if they were all pupil. She stood and
looked at me, her head on one side, like a
thrush considering how or where to dig at
his worm. Then she kissed me, and told me
all about it. 'I think I'm the happiest woman
in Europe,' she said. 'He's asked me to
marry him.' 'And what did you say?' I
asked her. She looked at me, her eyes laughing. 'I didn't say anything,' she said. 'There
wasn't time.' I say, he's an old corker, isn't
he though?"

I admitted that Sir Roderick might well
be a corker.

"Well, she simply drank in happiness by
the bosomful. She didn't understand that
it could be so awfully nice and not be bad for
you. 'Why don't I get drunk?' she said.
And then she said, 'Oh, I *will* be good to him!'
and then again, in a way that touched me,
'I've never had the chance of being good
before.' It was rot, you know; but I'm sure
that she felt like that."

I was not so sure that it was rot. I guessed
that the Baron had been thwarting to virtue.

Miss Bacchus allowed for the Baron. His

life had hardened him. He had no use for
good women and couldn't understand them.
His palate had been ruined. "All cayenne
pepper, you know," she said.

I ended up with a "Poor old Hector!"
But she said, "Pooh! She'll be awfully kind
to Hector. He don't want to marry anybody.
He only wants a woman to say his prayers to.
Will you take my three to one that he's his
father's best man?"
I said that I would not. And it was lucky
for me that I didn't. Because he was.

That's all over long ago. There's been a
child since, and they do say—— But the
child in being is a daughter, and called, with
great gallantry, Euphemia. So Sir Roderick
has tackled the Malleson curse, and looks
like winning.
But I remember that Pat—at the wedding
—had a gibe about Hector being like a mute
at his own funeral; and that afterwards,
when we had seen the happy pair off, and
were lighting up, he had taken my arm, with
the pretty wheedling way he had, and said,

"Don't you love a chap who's an ass *pour le bon motif?*" I admit that I do. I'm awfully fond of Hector; and he'll make an excellent stepson. Not that he will be asked to play Hippolytus. Helena is madly in love with her old Theseus. You never saw a fonder couple. Inseparable!

The Magic of Jewels and Charms

By GEORGE FREDERICK KUNZ, A.M., PH.D., D.SC.
With numerous plates in color, doubletone and line. Decorated cloth, gilt top, in a box. $5.00 net. Half morocco, $10.00
net. Uniform in style and size with " The Curious Lore of
Precious Stones." The two volumes in a box, $10.00 net.

It will probably be a new and surely a fascinating subject to which Dr. Kunz introduces the reader. The most
primitive savage and the most highly developed Cauca-
sian find mystic meanings, symbols, sentiments and, above
all, beauty in jewels and precious stones; it is of this magic
lore that the distinguished author tells us. In past ages
there has grown up a great literature upon the subject—
books in every language from Icelandic to Siamese, from
Sanskrit to Irish—the lore is as profound and interesting
as one can imagine. In this volume you will find the
unique information relating to the magical influence which
precious stones, amulets and crystals have been supposed
to exert upon individuals and events.

The Civilization of Babylonia and Assyria

By MORRIS JASTROW, JR., PH.D., LL.D. 140 Illustrations.
Octavo. Cloth, gilt top, in a box, $6.00 net.

This work covers the whole civilization of Babylonia
and Assyria, and by its treatment of the various aspects
of that civilization furnishes a comprehensive and complete survey of the subject. The language, history,
religion, commerce, law, art and literature are thoroughly
presented in a manner of deep interest to the general
reader and indispensable to historians, clergymen, anthro-
pologists and sociologists. The volume is elaborately
illustrated and the pictures have been selected with the
greatest care so as to show every aspect of this civilization,
which alone disputes with that of Egypt, the fame of
being the oldest in the world. For Bible scholars the
comparisons with Hebrew traditions and records will have
intense interest.

English Ancestral Homes of Noted Americans

By ANNE HOLLINGSWORTH WHARTON, Author of "In Chateau Land," etc., etc. 28 illustrations. 12mo. Cloth $2.00 net. Half morocco, $4.00 net.

Miss Wharton so enlivens the past that she makes the distinguished characters of whom she treats live and talk with us. She has recently visited the homelands of a number of our great American leaders and we seem to see upon their native heath the English ancestors of George Washington, Benjamin Franklin, William Penn, the Pilgrim Fathers and Mothers, the Maryland and Virginia Cavaliers and others who have done their part in the making of the United States. Although this book is written in an entertaining manner, and with many anecdotes and bypaths to charm the reader, it is a distinct addition to the literature of American history and will make a superb gift for the man or woman who takes pride in his or her library.

Heroes and Heroines of Fiction
Classical, Mediaeval and Legendary

By WILLIAM S. WALSH. Half morocco, Reference Library style, $3.00 net. Uniform with "Heroes and Heroines of Fiction, Modern Prose and Poetry." The two volumes in a box, $6.00 net.

The fact that the educated men of to-day are not as familiar with the Greek and Roman classics as were their fathers gives added value to Mr. Walsh's fascinating compilation. He gives the name and setting of all the anywise important characters in the literature of classical, mediæval and legendary times. To one who is accustomed to read at all widely, it will be found of the greatest assistance and benefit; to one who writes it will be invaluable. These books comprise a complete encyclopedia of interesting, valuable and curious facts regarding all the characters of any note whatever in literature. This is the latest addition to the world-famous Lippincott's Readers' Reference Library. Each volume, as published, has become a standard part of public and private libraries.

HEWLETT'S GREATEST WORK:
Romance, Satire and a German

The Little Iliad

By MAURICE HEWLETT. Colored frontispiece by Edward Burne-Jones. 12mo. $1.35 net.

A "Hewlett" that you and every one else will enjoy! It combines the rich romance of his earliest work with the humor, freshness and gentle satire of his more recent.

The whimsical, delightful novelist has dipped his pen in the inkhorn of modern matrimonial difficulties and brings it out dripping with amiable humor, delicious but fantastic conjecture. Helen of Troy lives again in the Twentieth Century, but now of Austria; beautiful, bewitching, love-compelling, and with it all married to a ferocious German who has drained the cup and is now squeezing the dregs of all that life has to offer. He has locomotor ataxia but that does not prevent his Neitschean will from dominating all about him, nor does it prevent Maurice Hewlett from making him one of the most interesting and portentous characters portrayed by the hand of an Englishman in many a day. Four brothers fall in love with the fair lady,—there are amazing but happy consequences. The author has treated an involved story in a delightful, naive and refreshing manner.

The Sea-Hawk

By RAPHAEL SABATINI. 12mo. Cloth. $1.25 net.

Sabatini has startled the reading public with this magnificent romance! It is a thrilling treat to find a vivid, clean-cut adventure yarn. Sincere in this, we beg you, brothers, fathers, husbands and comfortable old bachelors, to read this tale and even to hand it on to your friends of the fairer sex, provided you are certain that they do not mind the glint of steel and the shrieks of dying captives.

The Man From the Bitter Roots

By CAROLINE LOCKHART. 3 illustrations in color by Gayle Hoskins. 12mo. $1.25 net.

"Better than 'Me-Smith'"—that is the word of those who have read this story of the powerful, quiet, competent Bruce Burt. You recall the humor of "Me-Smith,"— wait until you read the wise sayings of Uncle Billy and the weird characters of the Hinds Hotel. You recall some of those flashing scenes of "Me-Smith"—wait until you read of the blizzard in the Bitter Roots, of Bruce Burt throwing the Mexican wrestling champion, of the reckless feat of shooting the Roaring River with the dynamos upon the rafts, of the day when Bruce Burt almost killed a man who tried to burn out his power plant,—then you will know what hair-raising adventures really are. The tale is dramatic from the first great scene in that log cabin in the mountains when Bruce Burt meets the murderous onslaught of his insane partner.

A Man's Hearth

By ELEANOR M. INGRAM. Illustrated in color by Edmund Frederick. 12mo. $1.25 net.

The key words to all Miss Ingram's stories are "freshness," "speed" and "vigor." "From the Car Behind" was aptly termed "one continuous joy ride." "A Man's Hearth" has all the vigor and go of the former story and also a heart interest that gives a wider appeal. A young New York millionaire, at odds with his family, finds his solution in working for and loving the optimistic nursemaid who brought him from the depths of trouble and made for him a hearthstone. There are fascinating side issues but this is the essential story and it is an inspiring one. It will be one of the big books of the winter.

RECENT VALUABLE PUBLICATIONS

The Practical Book of Period Furniture

Treating of English Period Furniture, and American Furniture of Colonial and Post-Colonial date, together with that of the typical French Periods.

By HAROLD DONALDSON EBERLEIN and ABBOTT Mc-CLURE. With 225 illustrations in color, doubletone and line. Octavo. Handsomely decorated cloth. In a box. $5.00 net.

This book places at the disposal of the general reader all the information he may need in order to identify and classify any piece of period furniture, whether it be an original, or a reproduction. The authors have greatly increased the value of the work by adding an illustrated chronological key by means of which the reader can distinguish the difference of detail between the various related periods. One cannot fail to find the book absorbingly interesting as well as most useful.

The Practical Book of Oriental Rugs

By DR. G. GRIFFIN LEWIS, Author of "The Mystery of the Oriental Rug." New Edition, revised and enlarged. 20 full-page illustrations in full color. 93 illustrations in doubletone. 70 designs in line. Folding chart of rug characteristics and a map of the Orient. Octavo. Handsomely bound. In a box. $5.00 net.

Have you ever wished to be able to judge, understand, and appreciate the characteristics of those gems of Eastern looms? This is the book that you have been waiting for, as all that one needs to know about oriental rugs is presented to the reader in a most engaging manner with illustrations that almost belie description. "From cover to cover it is packed with detailed information compactly and conveniently arranged for ready reference. Many people who are interested in the beautiful fabrics of which the author treats have long wished for such a book as this and will be grateful to G. Griffin Lewis for writing it." —*The Dial.*

The Practical Book of Outdoor Rose Growing

NEW EDITION
REVISED AND ENLARGED

By GEORGE C. THOMAS, JR. Elaborately illustrated with 96 perfect photographic reproductions in full color of all varieties of roses and a few half tone plates. Octavo. Handsome cloth binding, in a slip case. $4.00 net.

This work has caused a sensation among rose growers, amateurs and professionals. In the most practical and easily understood way the reader is told just how to propagate roses by the three principal methods of cutting, budding and grafting. There are a number of pages in which the complete list of the best roses for our climate with their characteristics are presented. One prominent rose grower said that these pages were worth their weight in gold to him. The official bulletin of the Garden Club of America said:—"It is a book one must have." It is in fact in every sense practical, stimulating, and suggestive.

The Practical Book of Garden Architecture

By PHEBE WESTCOTT HUMPHREYS. Frontispiece in color and 125 illustrations from actual examples of garden architecture and house surroundings. Octavo. In a box. $5.00 net.

This beautiful volume has been prepared from the standpoints of eminent practicability, the best taste, and general usefulness for the owner developing his own property,—large or small, for the owner employing a professional garden architect, for the artist, amateur, student, and garden lover. The author has the gift of inspiring enthusiasm. Her plans are so practical, so artistic, so beautiful, or so quaint and pleasing that one cannot resist the appeal of the book, and one is inspired to make plans, simple or elaborate, for stone and concrete work to embellish the garden.

Handsome Art Works of Joseph Pennell

The reputation of the eminent artist is ever upon the increase. His books are sought by all who wish their libraries to contain the best in modern art. Here is your opportunity to determine upon the purchase of three of his most sought-after volumes.

Joseph Pennell's Pictures of the Panama Canal

(Fifth printing) 28 reproductions of lithographs made on the Isthmus of Panama between January and March, 1912, with Mr. Pennell's Introduction giving his experiences and impressions, and a full description of each picture. Volume 7½ x 10 inches. Beautifully printed on dull finished paper. Lithograph by Mr. Pennell on cover. $1.25 net.

"Mr. Pennell continues in this publication the fine work which has won for him so much deserved popularity. He does not merely portray the technical side of the work, but rather prefers the human element."—*American Art News.*

Our Philadelphia

By ELIZABETH ROBINS PENNELL. Illustrated by Joseph Pennell. Regular Edition. Containing 105 reproductions of lithographs by Joseph Pennell. Quarto. 7½ x 10 inches. 552 pages. Handsomely bound in red buckram. Boxed. $7.50 net.

Autograph Edition. Limited to 289 copies (Now very scarce). Contains 10 drawings, reproduced by a new lithograph process, in addition to the illustrations that appear in the regular edition. Quarto. 552 pages. Specially bound in genuine English linen buckram in City colors, in cloth covered box. $18.00 net.

An intimate personal record in text and in picture of the lives of the famous author and artist in a city with a brilliant history, great beauty, immense wealth.

Life of James McNeill Whistler

By ELIZABETH ROBINS and JOSEPH PENNELL. Thoroughly revised Fifth Edition of the authorized Life, with much new matter added which was not available at the time of issue of the elaborate 2 volume edition, now out of print. Fully illustrated with 97 plates reproduced from Whistler's works. Crown octavo. 450 pages. Whistler binding, deckle edges. $3.50 net. Three-quarter grain levant, $7.50 net.

"In its present form and with the new illustrations, some of which present to us works which are unfamiliar to us, its popularity will be greatly increased."—*International Studio.*

The Stories All Children Love Series

This set of books for children comprises some of the most famous stories ever written. Each book has been a tried and true friend in thousands of homes where there are boys and girls. Fathers and mothers remembering their own delight in the stories are finding that this handsome edition of old favorites brings even more delight to their children. The books have been carefully chosen, are beautifully illustrated, have attractive lining papers, dainty head and tail pieces, and the decorative bindings make them worthy of a permanent place on the library shelves.

Heidi By JOHANNA SPYRI. Translated by Elisabeth P. Stork.

The Cuckoo Clock By MRS. MOLESWORTH.

The Swiss Family Robinson Edited by G. E. MITTON.

The Princess and the Goblin By GEORGE MACDONALD.

The Princess and Curdie By GEORGE MACDONALD.

At the Back of the North Wind By GEORGE MACDONALD.

A Dog of Flanders By "OUIDA."

Bimbi By "OUIDA."

Mopsa, the Fairy By JEAN INGELOW.

The Chronicles of Fairyland By FERGUS HUME.

Hans Andersen's Fairy Tales

Each large octavo, with from 8 to 12 colored illustrations. Handsome cloth binding, decorated in gold and color. $1.25 net, per volume.

CPSIA information can be obtained
at www.ICGtesting.com
Printed in the USA
LVHW051407110621
690002LV00010B/606